J.M.J.

Ad Maré

Song of the Pleiades

Grace Bourget

En Route Books and Media, LLC
Saint Louis, MO

⊕ENROUTE
Make the time

En Route Books and Media, LLC
5705 Rhodes Avenue
St. Louis, MO 63109

Contact us at
contact@enroutebooksandmedia.com

Cover Credit: Grace Bourget
Copyright 2024 Grace Bourget

ISBN-13: 979-8-88870-163-8
Library of Congress Control Number: 2024938961

Dedication

In memory of my mother, Lisa Bourget, who kept
me writing even when it seemed fruitless.

To the Sorrowful Heart of Our Lady of La Salette
&
The Holy Face of Jesus

~

For those who struggle to find purpose

~

For my spiritual brothers, Archangels Michael,
Gabriel, and Raphael

~

For Chantal and Claudia

"He shakes the earth from its place and makes its pillars tremble. He speaks to the sun and it does not shine; He seals off the light of the stars. He alone stretches out the heavens and treads on the waves of the sea. He is the Maker of Arcturus and Orion, the Pleiades and the constellations of the south." Job 9:6-9

"The waters are hardened like a stone, and the surface of the deep is congealed. Shalt thou be able to join together the shining stars the Pleiades, or canst thou stop the turning about of Arcturus? Canst thou bring forth the day star in its time, and make the evening star to rise upon the children of the earth?" - Job 38:30-32

"Seek Him that maketh Arcturus, and Orion, and that turneth darkness into morning, and that changeth day into night: that calleth the waters of the sea, and poureth them out upon the face of the earth:

The Lord is His name. He that with a smile bringeth destruction upon the strong, and waste upon the mighty." - Amos 5:8-9

Character List

<u>Pleia</u> – Orphaned Princess of the Temple.

<u>Eridan</u> – Warrior and Guardian of the Temple and the consecrated maidens there. Acts as an adopted brother to them, particularly Pleia.

<u>Dianthe</u> – One of the Temple maidens, the closest friend of Pleia. She took a temporary vow of silence in reparation.

<u>Arcturus</u> – One of the Kingdom's exiled Guardians, who had grown up alongside Eridan.

<u>Trissa</u> – Arc's sister.

<u>Elnath</u> – Queen of Celae, who overthrew her uncle, Antaré.

<u>Antaré</u> – Previous king and tyrant.

<u>Maia</u> – The name by which Mary is known in the Kingdoms. The Pleiades have been attributed to her in honor of her sorrows and joys.

<u>Scier</u> – The name by which Christ is known; the Daystar.

<u>Ireo</u> – The Archangel Gabriel, the Lily. His is the star Albireo.

<u>Tiran</u> – The Archangel Raphael, Life of Heaven. His is the star of Vega.

<u>Ascheré</u> – The Archangel Michael, the leader and Lord of the Mighty Stars. His is the star of Sirius.

Table of Contents

I
Epiphany

Water lapped methodically at the breaking dawn. The air was salty yet sweet, eddying with a breeze as cool as the waters seemed to be. Somewhere above, the hymn of a seagull, or was it an eagle? Rang out among the creaking timbers and comfortable shivering of heavy fabric which could have been that of a sail.

"Awaken, my little one," a woman's voice spoke softly, and Pleia opened her eyes.

She didn't wonder what she was doing on that boat, despite never having seen it before, and it wasn't the kind anyone used anymore.

For a moment, her eyes were finding the deep zaffre of the sea, rippled like fractured obsidian, and the rosy haze of the sky that was the blushing mauve and lilac of a winter rose, glowing with the amber of sunrise.

The boat was drifting unaided to a pier of marble with crystal lights.

Yet, as she noticed these things, she forgot them for the face of the woman who leaned over her so tenderly. Pleia knew her, or thought she did; but it wasn't her mother or anyone she knew back home.

Come to think of it, the thought of home was as foggy as the mist curling over the waves. She couldn't remember where that was; she almost couldn't remember who she knew.

Pleia looked up to the woman once more to meet a smile that hovered like a star over the evening mountaintops. Something about her seemed unearthly, like a transparent veil through which veins of brightest azure ran like breathless rivers, and echoes of ancient light lived deep within her eyes.

"Maia?"

The woman smiled again and rose, straightening her willowy frame so that the pleats of her glaucous robe rippled and pooled about her feet.

"Come and see."

There was something sad in those eyes, Pleia decided, as she arose, but she was not yet questioning any of these strange things. A gentle bump brought the ship up to the pier. She arose and stepped off.

A wide vale spread out before them, hung with a cloak of mist and dew, and sprung with quaint flowers that seemed like fairy stones.

The former curled all about, beginning to obscure the sea from view.

From somewhere came a sound which one might expect to hear if the amber of honey, raining waterfalls, and bells were all one and the same.

Pleia glanced up at the woman; it was hard to turn her eyes away. Before the girl could speak, the lady put a finger to her lips, with a tender look, and they went on.

The wet grass brushed their ankles yet did not cling as it normally would. Everything seemed still and serene.

The waves grew distant, but the shimmery sound seemed not far now. The vale began to slope, and a frosted city rose above them, spires lost among the stars. There were fireflies all about them now, glowing even in the morning light.

The city felt alive, but no one was there. Whenever Pleia turned her head, she thought she could see people before her, the way faint stars brighten in the corner of the eye.

Through a corridor of fountains and pillars, they came to a spacious courtyard. Here, spring-fed streams sang with songbirds, and vines were hung with unnamed flowers and frosted berries.

From there, Pleia could see, through the delicately-laced archways, the zaffre of the sea, and in the distance, the shadow of land: her land.

In the center of the garden lay a deep ovaline pool, ringed by lush moss, phyla, and smooth sea glass pearls, braced by twining vines. The water was the dark stillness of a sapphire.

Maia stood at the pool's edge and drew Pleia close.

To her surprise, seven stars glimmered within, singing, magnified as though they lived within; when she looked skywards, the faint stars were scattered across the sky, and those seven stars lived above, but were terribly far distant.

Maia laid her hands on Pleia's shoulders.

"This is the Star-Pool," she murmured. "These stars are yours, as they are mine. But for this treasure, you will suffer great sorrow, as I have. Even as the sea rolls between us, our stars will be your hope and will bring you back to me."

Pleia's eyes rose again to the shadow of land in the distance. It seemed to be flying closer and closer, until she could see dimly through the fog, the shadows of battle and hear the cries of men, women, and children.

"Maia?" She asked uncertainly, reaching for the lady's hand. "Am I dead? Is this Starra?"

Maia smiled, almost sorrowfully.

"No, my little one. This is a place which once was mine, and that of Scier, but it was taken away and plunged into a darkness which will soon cover your world. You are only asleep, little one. Soon you will be awakened."

Maia smoothed the child's hair.

"Do not fear, Pleia, I will always be near."

She bent and kissed Pleia's brow as the land whirled closer, and the island melted into the mist. A melody spun which would linger in her ears, and with it came a whisper.

Follow the Pleaides. . . Follow!

II

Prophecy

Pleia, princess of the Temple of the Daystar, stood on its terrace and wondered.

Follow the Pleiades. . . follow! Kept repeating more and more urgently in her mind. Unconsciously, she hummed the seven lilting notes which had become ingrained in her mind.

It had been seventeen years since Maia, Mother of Christ the Daystar, had kissed the little child's brow that fateful day.

The day when the kingdom fell.

The day when her parents had fallen alongside many families, leaving Pleia unconscious and undiscovered beneath a broken wagon.

When the battlefield had moved elsewhere, she had been found by a burial party. That was when the new mark, bright like a star on her brow, had taken her off the orphan's path and brought her to the Temple.

It had been centuries since a similar mark had been seen on the last Princess of the Temple. So, she had been taken under the Temple fathers' protection, and joined the sisters and other young maidens there in prayer. Some were consecrated virgins for life; others offered their lives in love until their kingdom could be freed from the darkness.

There Pleia had stayed and looked upon the Pleiades each night, waiting. Waiting for what, she wasn't quite sure. What she was sure of was the state of the Kingdom.

The events of seventeen years prior had lain at the foot of the throne, labeled with the name of Antaré, tyrant king, who had likely poisoned his half-brother to land the crown.

Only a year into his reign, he had plunged Celae into the deepest depression the kingdom had ever experienced; he had taxed to the point of bankrupting the majority of its citizens, stolen whatever was of value when the tax couldn't be paid, and promptly splurged all he had collected to add to his ego's possessions; to this he had responded by a massive inflation, both of himself and the Kingdom's coinage.

Further still, he had hurled the kingdom into a fruitless war with all of the surrounding kingdoms, striving to unite them under himself; exiled all the Kingdom's best who had opposed him, the Guardians who had long been Celae's protectors against an ancient curse; and the end result was that the entire land was compromised. Enemies were everywhere within and without, and it was they who had slaughtered the people all those years ago.

The darkness had fallen at the last stroke of his pen, when his sense of modernity had stripped the land of its religious love, its official allegiance to the Daystar, Scier, and to His mother, Maia, and all its laws of the love of God, neighbor, and truth.

The ancient kingdom's heart, a relic of the Great Star of Bethel, given by the angels, had been thought an eyesore and destroyed – why? In the end, to make heavy chains of gold and precious star-gems for Antaré to wear, and a throne of undue magnificence.

It had always been said that if the relic went, a tri-fold flood would come: darkness, invasion, and the sea. The light of Celae would vanish and be filled with the darkness of sorrow; and upon the night of October's new moon, seventeen years from thence, poison would drain the veins of the warring kingdoms. When nothing was left, the sea would come to claim it to a watery grave.

There was a remedy, they had always said, too, but no one had thought such a thing would come to pass, and all neglected to remember anything about it.

Yes, Antaré had been a king like no other in Celae's history, those long twenty years of his reign. When his niece, Elnath, had finally risen to the throne and exiled him, the laws were reinstated, but little else could be done. The kingdom had been left in shambles, the population cut by a quarter.

Yes, darkness had covered the kingdom, both in state and in effect, for the clouds had closed overhead, and only parted to reveal the night sky. Famine had been widespread until innovations were made, and some sunlight plants could now grow under false light, but now, most foods produced were those which bloomed by starlight.

The stars were shining above Pleia now, among the jeweltones of a lonely nightingale. It brought back a song to her mind, one she seemed to sing endlessly after her awakening, and she began to murmur it, softly.

"Remember, Morning Star, O Heaven's light,
How thy Son is our Starbright. . .
Let your stars shine for me

> *To you I give my heart,*
> *Hear my plea,*
> *Cast a glance beyond the sea!"*

"Pleia?"

The maiden turned her head.

"Eridan."

"You've been out long, little Pleia. The curfew remains for your safety."

The young man came and stood at the balustrade beside her. Eridan Cadoret was the Warrior-Keeper of the Temple, champion of the Kingdom, and guardian of the virgins. Under Antaré, Eridan had been ordered away many times, always to return despite it and only in time to prevent the virgins from being forcefully dispersed.

Now that Elnath, the true heir to the throne, had deposed the tyrant, things were better. But Celae was still in tatters, and the sky was still gray; enemies brewed war on every side, and fear had scattered hope.

"You are grave tonight, dear one; what is troubling you?"

"The dream has been relentless for a fortnight now," Pleia murmured. "She keeps telling me now to follow the Pleiades. I feel her calling me to go now, and yet I don't know how."

Eridan leaned upon the balustrade.

"I feel you are right, my sister. I have been called to the palace on the morrow, and I am to bring you with me before Lady Elnath."

Pleia stopped. She hadn't left the Temple grounds since that day. She read the same thoughts in Eridan's eyes.

"You had best get some sleep now. I think you're going to need it."

He offered her his arm and they went inside, through the candlelit corridors with their soft, shimmering shadows, until the door to Pleia's royal chamber stood before them.

"Dream well of Maia," Eridan said softly, "and worry not about her call. You won't be alone."

He touched her face tenderly and bade her good night. The stars shone on, and the night waned as the Temple fell silent, save for the sound of the lone nightingale.

III

Entreaty

Fog pervaded the streets of Tygeta as the pure white steeds picked their way up the hill. Early morning had left a coat of dew dripping from the ivied walls and pearling on Pleia's gray mantle.

Eridan rode closely by, keeping his eyes on the street ahead while his stallion listened to sounds echoing faintly down the alleyways.

Wash was being hung, not that the sun would help it dry, and children were creeping out to play and wonder at such errant visitors.

The star on Pleia's brow was difficult to hide. Even the shadow of her deep hood could not darken its frostiness. The women in the windows whispered, and smiled down, and the men setting out to work stopped to wonder.

Yet, one never knew what shadow haunted the streets. It was no wonder that Eridan suffered to be alert and was silently glad when the palace grounds were safely beneath the horses' hooves.

Elnath awaited her guests in the Constellarium. There was, after all, no use in solariums.

She stood tall under the deep cobalt wings of the ceiling, where constellations were marked in silver and gold during the day and parted at night to frame the sky.

The iced strawberry curls, hallmark of the family, were unusually let loose over her shoulders, and the circles beneath her eyes told the tale of a restless night. Elnath greeted them with warmth, but wearily.

Eridan bowed before her and drew Pleia forward.

"The Daystar's Princess, my lady."

"Ah," Elnath murmured as Pleia shook back her hood. "It has long been my wish to speak with you, favored Pleia."

Her eyes wandered over the star-sign.

"It is good to see the world again a little, I would suppose, even in this troubled kingdom. Come and study the stars with me, and I shall tell you why I have summoned you hither."

She moved to the center of the room, where the bright gem Vega would have been shining. Infinitesimal gears in the thousands moved the false sky, tick by tick, millimeter by millimeter, so that ever the stars were in their true placement. Their magnitude, too, echoed what would be seen.

Elnath spoke.

"The world grows darker by the moment."

Her eyes were on the shifting stars which twinkled soberly in reply.

"You know of the curses which the tyrant – my uncle – brought down upon us. Both the metaphysical and physical in nature. Our kingdom stands to be defeated on all sides, and by day and by night there are secret enemies slipping through our borders. They know no darkness but that which is internal and that which is natural."

"Strength lies in innovation, as well," Pleia said quietly. "Our people have much strength which the enemy does not possess."

Elnath smiled.

"As wise as you are young."

She went to a portrait that hung in an alcove in the north of the room. It was of a maiden a few years younger than Pleia, but whose brow was marked with the same star.

"The last time the star was seen, Rána, the bearer, was the savior of our people, a tamer of the monsters which hunted our ancestors."

Elnath turned to Pleia.

"You are my last hope! Help my people, I plead! Has He called you? Have you been waiting all this time? Tell me, Pleia, can you help us?"

Pleia opened her mouth and the story poured out in ways she had never described to anyone.

As Elnath listened, the sorrow in her eyes was replaced by a whisper of hope.

"Yet, how does one follow the Pleiades?" she inquired, when Pleia had ceased to speak.

Pleia lifted her eyes to find the star cluster where it lay, brightly beaded above her.

"Like an arrow, to follow the direction in which it aligns. If the time is now, we shall follow to the northwest. By day, an estimation in accord with a compass should suffice."

"Nay," Lady Elnath interposed. "The Constellarium in travel form will be of assistance here."

"Pleia," Eridan said, "I think there is a fact we neglect. As the Pleiades rise and fall, the direction of its arrow is in constant redirection and would have one backtracking in the end, for if it rises pointing northwest, once it sets it shall point to the southeast. Traveling at night would be dangerous, and so, then, which way would one go?"

Pleia considered this carefully. "I think, with the Constellarium's help, one would follow during the day the direction given by the Pleiades at its rising. If one cannot see it on the other face of the earth, one cannot truly be expected to follow it, I think."

"Seems wise enough," Elnath mused.

She raised her head and placed her left hand on Pleia's shoulder.

"I ask you, Pleia, daughter of Maia and Princess of the Daystar, take all that you need and go, for the sake of our Light and our Kingdom. Heed the Lady's call and follow the Pleiades."

"Find the Guardians, for they know the life of travel, and the land, better than all others. Do what you are able to bring back their trust."

"Eridan, accompany her. If a guardian guides her, make your judgment, whether you will remain or return. I know in the past your departure from the Temple was foreboding to the Virgins, and so, while you are away, my own champion, trustworthy and pure of heart, will protect them in your stead. Will you do this?"

Eridan and Pleia understood now what they were going to go through. They exchanged a silent glance and accepted the hand that was being held out to each.

Morning came, still and dark; a bird sang, and its song echoed through the city and the valley below, bringing other voices into the clear air like a spark leaping among firewood and igniting. The rivers gleamed snow and gold like the clearest sunlit diamonds strewn over paths of silver, and the autumn leaves glowed like fire in the morning light.

Preparations were made; provisions were gathered, over and above need if circumstances should arise; the hand-held Constellarium was given to Pleia, and traveling wardrobes fitted. Elnath had a leather coronet of pleasing design made and fitted it to Pleia's brow; thus, would it offer protection, the Lady said, for such a star as the maiden's would call down as much evil upon her shoulders as good.

Eridan and Pleia would travel northwards on the morrow, into the territory of the Guardians: the deep woodland which ringed Celae all about like a shield.

Whether the Guardians would reveal themselves as friend, foe, or not at all, was a question which Eridan found weighed heavily on his mind.

Pleia found her sleep to be dreamless that night and worried.

Word was sent back to the Temple, and Eridan's replacement was met, found trustworthy, and sent on his way.

It was scarcely a noticeable dawn when Elnath stood upon the palace gateway and watched Eridan and the maid go.

No news had been given to anyone in the land, lest unfounded hopes be sprung, or unfriendly ears hear.

Pleia's eyes roved the countryside as it crept onward before them; it was beautiful enough despite the oncoming rain, but she still remembered the last day when she had ridden down such a road. She pulled up her mare sharply enough for Alcyone to whinny.

"Dianthe?"

A maid only a little younger than she sat laughing silently from the saddle of her own silver-dappled filly, barring the road.

"Dianthe Esmond!" Eridan echoed, severely. "What are you doing, little maid? You're hardly intended to be here."

Dianthe raised her hands and signed, *I may have followed you. . . .*

"All this time? Dianthe! You're a dedicated maiden, not to leave the Temple until the light returns. I hardly see it yet. You didn't even have my protection."

Dianthe signed once more.

Pleia isn't the only one who dreams.

Yet she looked pleadingly apologetic.

Pleia laughed as the rain began to fall, and nudged Alcyone closer. Leaning from the saddle, she embraced Dianthe.

"You really ought to stop following me, Dia, but I am glad you have not."

Eridan sighed, studying the clouds. He raised his hood.

"I'll send word to the Temple that they're not to worry about you. Hood up, Dia, you always were a reckless one."

But he smiled as he pressed his stallion, 'Ega, into a trot and waved the maidens after him. Pleia's laughter trailed on the wind as Dianthe filled the falling rain with the sound of her silent chatter.

IV
Chivalry

Two evenings later. . .

The forest was coming onwards now, looming dark and statuesque in the gathering moonlight. Eridan called a halt and took his charges into the nearest inn, herding them up the back stairs. The dangers of the forest would have to wait until daylight.

Their road would lead them through the forest of Archidron, through the ruins of the ancient gates. The only way to find the Guardians would be to let the Guardians find the intruders first.

Morning dawned cold and wet, and the roads were flooded. Yet, there was some safety in that whatever lay in the trees might endeavor to remain dry and the travelers might remain unmolested.

Might.

There were monsters in the forest, bears and wolves of strange breed, likely descendants of those tamed by the previous Princess.

23

Then there were the foes: raiding parties, scouts, and assassins, which slipped through the wood. No one in Celae knew how many times the Guardians had turned those evildoers back.

The eternal fog curled above the leaves that squelched underfoot and fell thickly through the branches before them, limiting their vision. The rain was letting up.

A bird crowed from somewhere overhead. Twigs snapped under the horses' hooves. The pine trees were all obsidian in color, and the maples were deep wine in the dim light.

Broken stones like snapped limbs rose out of the fog, bringing back Eridan's memories of a gate which saw sunshine and peace, and outsiders passed freely, no bitter curse to be held by. And he remembered when the Guardians had been his family.

Eridan felt a creeping sensation in the back of his head.

Something was moving through the trees before them. Its breath was heavy, and so were the muffled footfalls.

'Ega pulled back and Eridan backed him up, motioning for the maids to do the same. The broken walls of the gatehouse braced them on all sides now – safe, or a trap.

Pleia reached out and clasped Dianthe's wrist; the latter's hands were shaking enough to make the filly doubly nervous. Dianthe might have been reckless, but it didn't mean she was never afraid.

Eridan's eyes darted across the small visible stretch before them. Whatever was there seemed to be moving in all directions at once. He was deeply regretting having brought Pleia and Dianthe with him, not that it could have been helped.

The sounds ceased.

A soft creak of leather as Eridan's weight shifted, as though he were seeing without seeing. His sword was still in its sheath, but the shield was tightened on his forearm.

A yell and a hulking shadow crashed out of the mist -

'Ega's head swung down, Eridan's shield swung up, and the gaping jaws crashed against it, sending shudders ripping through the nerves in tooth and arm.

Dianthe's filly reared. The maiden tumbled out of the saddle.

The bear reared out of the whiteness, descendant of titans, three times the size of the great bears in the north; its claws two hands in length, and ram-like horns spiraled on either side of the skull, able to crush, scatter and destroy anything in its way.

Blood spattered across Eridan's shield, dripping from the creature's raw gums, in which were set rotting teeth.

Hellacious eyes turned xanthic as the bear recovered from the stun. Eridan's sword flashed – it was a poor match against massive, daggered paws, but there was a reason it was he who was champion, and none other.

Pleia leapt from Alcyone's back, shoving her and the filly back under the wall's overhang, not sure if it would hold against the bear's weight, should it fall; and she grabbed Dianthe, pulling her to her feet.

'Ega was dancing, hooves flying as he nimbly dodged heavy paws and head. Eridan kept the bear from charging, nicking face and chest so that its fur dripped wet. If the bear once thrusted its head and caught the blade, it could be the end.

Pleia realized why they had felt surrounded.

"'Dan, look out!" she cried, and the group split, diving in opposite directions as a second, sable-matted bear plunged down from behind.

'Ega leapt the crumbled wall and the bears crashed head to head with the sound of shattering stone as their horns met solidly.

But now, the maidens were trapped, and Eridan found himself blocked. Only if he could draw the beasts' attention to himself, and not the easier prey, two for one target -

He yelled, striking the flat of his blade upon his shield, the sound ringing through the trees.

Both heads turned.

The filly whinnied in fear.

The sable one swung around and the first lumbered toward Eridan, leaving him no opening.

Pleia snatched Dianthe's arm.

"Through the window!"

There was a pane-less window behind them, unblocked. She shoved the girl through the broken frame and seized the horses' reins. If they didn't get the horses safe somehow, they wouldn't be able to simply ride out of danger.

Something in her was helplessly hoping that she had something of her predecessor's knack with monsters, but what was it? It wasn't forthcoming.

"Pleia!" Eridan shouted. "*Down!*"

She realized those yellow eyes were bearing down on her and she was staring into open jaws.

She dropped and let the horses run.

The wall behind her crumbled as the bear narrowly missed Pleia. Rubble tumbled down around Dianthe, trapping her.

The battle was interrupted by the blaring of a horn, but Eridan's still hung at his side. A rush of pounding steps and four riders sailed into the fray: two armored men on horseback and two young warriors on strange steeds: a golden-coated bear smaller in size, with a crown of horn, deerlike, and a mammoth doe with horse-like tail and feathered hooves, her nimble leaps keeping the danger at bay.

Her rider, a young woman, drew her bow and sent an obsidian-edged arrow into the skull of Eridan's foe.

"Good shot!" Eridan exclaimed as the bear spun round with a bellow, giving the champion the opening to lunge and cleave one horn from its head.

The girl spun her stave in reply and continued to weave in and out of the bear's reach, drawing it out into the open and joining Eridan's fight.

Two smaller bears, the riders' companions, ducked through the beasts' legs, forming distracting trip-hazards.

The bear-rider had vaulted from its back and blocked the sable bear's path to Pleia, for while the collision had led it to stumble backwards, Pleia had no room to run.

The bear bared its teeth at the new nuisance and raised one paw to sideswipe the guardian out of its way.

The stranger snapped his arms forward as in a shield, but a click, and a dozen hornet-stung, tooth-like darts launched from the carven plates on his arms and embedded inches deep into the monster's chest.

With one hand, the man swung Pleia aside as the bear charged; his mount drove his sharp antlers into the monster's side, forcing it to twist its path, and the man drove his spear into its mark.

The two horse riders had been dancing through the fray, offering openings and making them, and one had caught up with Dianthe from the broken wall.

The first bear, now hornless, received a painful gash when it caught Eridan's blade in its jaws, only for the warrior to rake it through the gap between its teeth. Eyes blurred by pain, the bear recoiled, swinging head up out of reach – leaving itself tragically vulnerable for the only moment needed.

Both bears fell silent in the same moment.

A minute passed as everyone caught their breath.

Everyone but the woman dismounted. One of the men brought the horses out of the trees and gave the reins to Pleia. She checked on Dianthe as her defender retrieved his weaponry. Eridan cleansed his sword and unbuckled his shield.

The Guardian shook his head a little and pushed back his dark hair. He was tall and clad in the russet and olive colors of his people, and his cloak was clasped by a six-pointed golden star; his eyes were dark and serious, though he seemed silently exhilarated by the battle.

"Didn't imagine doing that this morning. . . Oh and! Good morning."

Pleia gave a little laugh. "It's hardly been a pleasant one."

"Clearly."

"Perhaps you should have said simply, morning?"

Now it was the ranger's turn to laugh, and he admitted that she had a point.

Pleia thanked him.

"For what?" he asked. "Sending those beasts to the land they belong to? It was my pleasure. But you're welcome." He studied her keenly for a moment more.

One of the men raised his voice and addressed Pleia's defender. "Arc, Alula's injured. Alkaid's fine, but they'd best get back to Tania."

The man was bending over the smaller of the maroon-coated bears, feeling a damaged paw.

The Guardian, Arc, made a soft growling sound in his throat and both bears answered. Alkaid rose and stretched his left paw in the air as in a salute, put his shoulder to Alula's, and they trundled back into the trees.

"'Dan?" Pleia called softly. The horses and Dia were well; the blood coating Eridan's leather jerkin was troubling. "Are you hurt?"

Eridan glanced away from the Guardian he had been staring at.

"Barely, little one."

His gaze turned back to the Guardian who had swiveled to face him.

"Arc - that wouldn't happen to be short for Arcturus, now, would it?" Eridan drawled.

"'Dan wouldn't happen to be attached to Eri, would it?" Arcturus ducked around his mount and met Eridan's gaze with a little smile. They clasped hands.

"It's been too long," Eridan said.

"Far too long," Arcturus echoed. "I must say, your sense of impropriety hasn't changed much, if you're going to travel straight through Archidron and into enemy territory. With such companions, I might add."

"Well, I'm not the one who talks to bears."

"Well, I'm not the one who's stuck in a building guarding a dozen virgins all day."

"At least I get to be in the Temple all the time."

"True, but I find Him closer out in creation somehow, though I admit that being in the Temple would be pleasant. What are you doing out here? You didn't exactly choose the most inconspicuous mounts, though I give you points for hiding in the mist."

"Forgive me, but you don't have the most inconspicuous mounts, either." Eridan nodded at the bear standing at Arc's elbow.

Arcturus smiled a little and rubbed the bear's muzzle.

"Ur and Ceri are descendants of the creatures tamed by the Star-bound. Unlike these -" he jerked his head towards the two fallen beasts. "They remained tame. But these we have fought are evil in heart. For my sister Trissa's sake, we've been after them for almost a week now. They've caused her too much grief. There are times when I wish that the Star-Bound you protect in the Temple had the same gift and could cleanse these woods of their darkness."

Arc watched as Trissa dismounted the doe and wrested her arrows from the carcass at her feet. Her brother drove his spearhead into the ground to cleanse the blood from it.

Eridan eyed him. "Is that so. . . Pleia, you need not wear that here."

Pleia came forward, slipping the leather band from her brow. The Guardians stopped. Some of the pain left Trissa's face. Arcturus drew a sharp little breath and almost sighed, almost frowning in gravity.

Ur gave a happy whuffing sound, and both he and Ceri came and laid their muzzles in Pleia's hands.

"You'd best come now with us," Arc said quietly. "We must not allow any foul eyes to fall upon her, and there are too many in these woods."

V

Security

The sunken glade where the Northern Guardians dwelt was free of mist when the travelers arrived. A palisade of the kings of trees rose up on the walls about, extending the verdant canopy overhead; their roots wove a sturdy, tangled barricade draped with moss and vines, such that no man could ever get through, save through the Guardians' hidden tunnels.

Homes of shackled stone and timber were bound under mossy overhangs, and children ran barefoot through the grass and flowers.

Pathways of stepping-stone wandered through the village of Tania, skipping over brooks and passing by the compact gardens. The forest gave them everything they had.

Sometimes, it took away all that was good.

As Pleia's eyes wandered the glade, she found a cemetery, and within it nestled a new grave, far smaller than one ever should be. She closed her eyes and prayed.

Arcturus led the group to Tania's center, where a fire had been laid to disrupt the chill and prepare a meal for the returning parties. The men at once set about properly cleaning and preparing their equipment for their next use. Armor was removed, polished, and set aside.

Trissa did the same, but did not remove her leather guard, and the hard look in her eyes only dissipated when looking to her brother, or to the star on Pleia's brow.

The women were given seats by the fire on carven logs and looked after while they waited, yet the silence was one of procrastination, and Pleia could feel the glances of Tania's inhabitants falling upon her brow.

Arcturus went to his sister and rubbed her shoulders.

"You alright?" he asked softly, as though it meant in one manner and not in any other.

She nodded slowly and dropped her head against his chest. He hugged her.

"Do you need anything?"

Trissa hesitated.

"May I sit with you?" she asked finally.

"You never need to ask."

He took her and they sat down together on a log adjacent to the newcomers. Arcturus took a deep breath and exhaled, yet still he waited, arm around Trissa.

The other men – five now, three from another party – sat sharpening their swords. The only sound was that of blade on stone and a running brook. Arc looked again to his sister.

"It'll help," she murmured.

He pressed her fingers and turned at last to Eridan and his charges.

"As our guests you may remain in Tania as long as you need. Tell us now why you are here, whither you are going – and why the Star-Bound is outside the safety of the Temple's walls."

Eridan sheathed his sword and set it aside.

"Lady Elnath sent us, and yet, not by her command, but by Maia's. The Star-Bound will tell her tale in greater detail if you so desire; but she has been called to follow the Pleiades; on our way, Lady Elnath adjured us to find your people and make peace with you on her behalf. And if you will, to obtain a guard and guide for Pleia and the maid. If it is not agreeable to you, then I will continue to fill that role."

Arcturus looked upon them in turn as the other men waxed silent from the sharpening of their weaponry.

"It is ever the will of the Guardians to know what they are getting themselves into before it is begun," he said at length. "And I would have the second matter first, if you will. For there are far more dangers in these woods than anyone knows, as my sister Trissa could attest to."

He hastily laid his hand on Trissa's shoulder as she arose from her place.

"You need not, Trissa, I was merely saying."

She turned her eyes from the distant cemetery's knoll, fingers tightening around the curve of her leather weapon-belt.

"I had a child!"

Trissa's voice was trembling with rage and pain, and so were her hands, clenched at her sides, as she stared into the fire's glowing heart.

"I had a child! Until they came through . . . these monsters which we have battled this day. They took her from me when she wandered far. Without the light, these woods are dark, and all that is within them!"

She stormed off and went to the little grave beneath the trees.

Arc's aching heart was in his eyes as he watched his sister.

"She wasn't supposed to have that child," he said softly. "There are more dangers in these woods than beasts, and our women and children bear the worst of it."

His voice was bitter now.

"It wasn't her fault she was hurt, but Ayeleth gave her healing."

He looked away.

"These woods! These cursed woods, where we're trapped, where we can't protect our own – at times I wish the crown would fall. If Elnath is better than her uncle, where is our freedom?"

"Perhaps she had more to do in the beginning," Eridan said quietly.

His eyes followed Trissa with a softness that Pleia noticed, one which she had seen in his eyes years before, when he was only eight, and she, three. It was the day she had been found; he had been an acolyte and page to his father then. His father had been a Guardian, and Arc and Trissa Tähevӓli had been closer to him than friends.

"Elnath wishes to free you from your exile. Your people have suffered much and needlessly. It was only the tyrant who despised your presence. It is Elnath's wish that you accept the hospitality of the royal village of Nazar, where your women and children will be as safe as may be."

"And this in exchange for aid?"

"Nay. The rest is up to you; this is to right the wrongs of Antaré. You need do nothing when you've done more than anyone knows."

Arcturus tilted his head and gazed into the fire with folded arms.

"There are only five hundred of us men in these woods," he said slowly. "If we leave it, the only barrier to your realm will be the beasts of fickle mind."

He raised his head and studied each of his fellow Guardians in turn. They were nodding slowly.

"It is up to each camp," Arc said, picking up a log and feeding the fire. "I cannot speak for them all, only for Tania. Our gentle ones we will escort to safety. But in these woods will we remain, until no threat to our loved ones remains. As for your quest-"

He met Pleia's gaze and stopped, turning away again.

"We cannot let them wander through the wild."

It was Trissa who spoke, standing now at Eridan's shoulder. The anger had left her face. Eridan turned and offered her his hand. She took it.

"If a man may not be spared, let me go. I would not find the walls of Nazar safer than these trees. I know a little of the country into which they go. We may need the Pleiades as much as they."

Arc was silent as he belted his blade. His eyes met theirs, and the gravity fell away, replaced by the mischievous exhilaration which Eridan had once known.

"We leave at dawn."

VI

Westerly

Rush and river, ford and glen watched, whispering, as the company passed through. Bear, deer and horse all picked their way quietly through the unsettled outskirts of enemy territory.

They were traveling through the wild, cutting through barren regions of Uthold and Adar. It was nearly two weeks that they spent in the wild, as September neared its end. They had encountered no one; with Trissa's knowledge of old fields which had once belonged to Celae, and Arcturus' Guardian habits, they were able to pass safely undetected.

Eridan kept careful watch over his charges, for he had, almost unsurprisingly, chosen to remain. One man to three women was not as safe for them as could be, he and Arcturus had agreed. Though the latter had questioned how long Eridan could leave the Temple unguarded; to which the champion had mused that without Antaré, and with Elnath's own guard taking over, the virgins should not be in danger of dispersing. Or so he hoped, as his eyes fell on

Trissa's troubled face. Arcturus saw it and questioned no more.

When night fell, the men would set about making camp in the place chosen, making a shelter of branches, rushes, and greenery to conceal them from any wandering eyes. They'd use warming stones, rather than the tell-tale dangers of flame, and Pleia and Dia would aid with setting out a meal. Trissa always busied herself tending the animals.

One such evening, the wind was blowing across the rush-field, whistling through the hollow reeds and causing them to stir into each other rhythmically. Trissa stood well out of the reach of the dim glow of the stones. Clasping her arms, she searched the restless field with her eyes. Eridan came and stood beside her.

"I feel something out there," Trissa said, without turning.

Eridan likewise scanned the area, listening through the whistling.

"It's eerie, but I sense nothing," he murmured finally. "Don't forget, we have a man who talks to bears. If anyone can keep you safe. . ."

"And I don't forget that we have you."

Yet Trissa remained listening uneasily, her shoulders tense.

Eridan gently touched her right, his arm steady behind her. Trissa finally tore her eyes away from the night and let her shoulders rest against him.

"I wish it hadn't been so long, 'Dan. I liked the way it was, with the three of us. But it didn't work. Scier wanted it this way."

"I know. And I know why you're afraid," Eridan whispered. "Any beast out there will learn to fear, and any man out there would die if he so much as touched your hand unbidden. Both Arcturus and I would see to that."

Trissa sighed and leaned her head back on his shoulder, examining the faint sparkle of the Pleiades.

"I know. I just - you'd think the light of Starra would have penetrated everyone by now." She dropped her head. "No one makes any sense."

"I wish I could have been here. I wish that you never had to be here. There are a lot of things I wish, but I'm here now and I'll do the best by you that I can."

"There are many regrets I own, but I don't regret Ayeleth," Trissa muttered. "I'll never regret Ayeleth. She was my angel. . . she made up for all the sorrow."

"Then think of her playing with the stars now. . . she'd want you to."

A smile crossed the maiden's face.

"She would."

They listened to the wind once more.

"Still," she said abruptly, settling her shoulders anxiously. "I feel something out there. There's something there, 'Dan."

Eridan gently took her shoulders.

"Then we should be in camp. Come, Triss."

He took her back through the woven screen. They found Dianthe weaving plaits of wild grain by the fire and met Arcturus and Pleia, likewise returning from a look at the Pleiades.

Ur and Ceri seemed relieved to see them all; the horses were already asleep. It would seem that the plaits of grasses were for them, for quite a pile was accumulating, and a bag was ready to be filled; Dia had rubbed them with the oil of crushed rosemary and dipped them in the gel-sap of the fruit of the Asterose. They would be green and sweet for some time, should food become scarce.

"Trissa thinks something is out there," Eridan told them, taking a seat on the ground across from

Dia. "I didn't sense anything, but we should stay within these screens tonight."

Arc nodded, respectfully withdrawing his arm from Pleia's and giving her his cloak for a cushion.

"I felt something, too. I can't hear anything over the wind, but something is moving out there. A night creature, cats, perhaps. These fields make good homes for mice."

Trissa said nothing, but almost smiled when Arc came to sit beside her, humming an old song in her ear.

One by one, they drifted off to sleep while the men took turns keeping watch. The night remained uneventful save for the whispering in the field.

Rising early, the travelers rode through the restless reeds; they would cut through the marsh on the other side, and the worst of their journey would likely be over. They would be near the sea in just a day or two.

Trissa and Arcturus went to scout for a way around, but there was none. The marsh spread for miles north and south, like a river. They regrouped. Arcturus checked the sky. The usual gloom – for this had been Celaean territory before the war – was being darkened by storm clouds.

"If we send our mounts back now, they'll make it out of the storm's reach, Dia."

Dia blinked. Indeed, she didn't want her animal friends to become drenched, but send them back?

"They won't be able to navigate the swamp, little one, particularly Ur and 'Ega. Their weight will quickly discover pockets of death sand."

Trissa noted the maid's anxiety.

"Pockets of sand and mud covered by a thin crust. They're impossible to spot, save for the tiny sandblooms that give them away. Sometimes. The weight of any of the horses would send them sinking, and I'm not sure we could pull them out. If one of us, on the other hand, has the misfortune of a misstep, it won't be so bad."

Arcturus began unbuckling saddlebags and harnesses.

"So, whenever we come back, we're walking home," Pleia surmised.

"We're walking home."

Pleia squeezed Dianthe's hand as they exchanged troubled looks. That meant that two weeks would likely become four on the return journey.

"We'll get back in time," Eridan soothed. "Scier always gives enough time. Come now, put on your coats. It's growing chilly, and it's bound to get wet."

He aided them and joined Arc and Trissa in unbuckling saddles and bridles, leaving only a note hung around Ceri's neck, so the Guardians wouldn't worry at the mounts' return. It took some doing to convince the beasts that it was alright to depart, and they trotted off only reluctantly.

The plaited grains remained packed; in a pinch, they could be ground into bread, being equally edible for the travelers as for the horses.

"The marsh won't cross itself," Arcturus declared, shouldering a few of the packs. He gently swatted Pleia's hands away as she tried to take one from him. "We ought to get through it by nightfall, if possible."

They proceeded, following thin trails through waving grasses and pockets of water. It was almost noon when, nearing the end of the marsh, Dianthe froze.

Pleia glanced back.

"Dia, come! What is it?"

Dianthe was listening intently, turning her head from side to side. The others stopped when they realized the maids weren't following. Dianthe seized Pleia's hand and dragged her to the ground.

Five hundred pounds of cat, claws extended, missed them by mere inches, coming down over their heads with a snarl.

Trissa whipped out her bow and fired a warning shot at its feet. It only grasped the arrow in its teeth and snapped it in defiance as Dia and Pleia struggled to their feet and took the moment of distraction to dart through the reeds.

Pleia pushed Dia ahead of her as Eridan and Arcturus drew their weapons and blocked the way for the cat.

"Go! Start running!" Eridan called over his shoulder.

Trissa hesitated, then waved the maidens after her and they ran. They could hear the growling of a second cat as the men began weaving through the marsh, drawing the first away even as they ran. The women didn't get far.

Running in the marsh with the distraction of a wildcat was a recipe for disaster, and none had the time to watch for death sand, even if they had the ability to recognize it at that pace. It was Trissa who saw it first, but she was the one in its path and it was only a split-second before she was upon it.

The crust crumbled beneath her feet and plunged her into the sand up to her waist.

At once, the maids stopped to pull her out – the men running up, Arc threw himself flat and let one of the cats sail over his head as he yanked his sister out of the sand. Thankfully, that patch of sand extended far enough to catch that cat, rendering it out of the chase.

"Here comes the second – run!" Trissa panted, and off they went, breaking out of the marsh.

They found themselves faced by an endless field of brittle brambles. Worse, they were the ones featured in many of Adar's fairytales, for once the thorns were embedded in the skin, energy was drained until sleep came. Only when those thorns were removed or dissolved in the bloodstream would the victim be able to function once more.

Trissa stumbled in hesitation, but only for a moment. The thorns might be their safety yet.

"They won't follow us in!" she said. "Follow me, but don't get pricked!"

She ducked through a narrow tunnel in the branches. Eridan pushed the maids after her and they all went through, not a moment too soon. Claws raked the thorns where their heads had been only a moment before. The snarls followed them, growing wearied until they were silenced.

"Sounds like he'll have a purrfectly lovely nap," Arc commented as they began to pick their way gingerly through the briars.

"There should be a well somewhere in the center of the field," Trissa mused.

She stopped, looking around. There were no paths save ones paved by small rodents.

"Well, hopefully we'll come to it, but if not, we'll just continue after the Pleiades."

It didn't take long for the group to become hopelessly separated. For a time, Pleia was alone. Her heart beat anxiously for the others, never minding that she was surrounded by briars. Finding a trampled track, she hunted down Arcturus, who laughed softly at her distress and kept her close.

They found themselves wandering in vain, swatting grasses out of the way, cautiously, for a branch of thorn might be anywhere within that wave of the arm. Strange ebonized vines twisted across the ground, and these seemed to be the briars' roots.

Sometimes, Pleia was certain that they looped themselves around her feet, when they had been harmlessly out of her way, and would have caused her to fall into a thorny nest. If not for Arcturus, she would have been drained many times over.

The pair had backtracked briefly to search for the others, but having no luck, hoped no one had fallen asleep and knew they'd all reach the other side eventually. That is, as long as everyone continued west and neither north nor south. Trissa and Eridan would be able to keep direction well. Dia – just so long as no one let go of her hand and let her get lost, she'd be alright.

The wind was picking up again and the storm was coming on quickly; they could hear the building rumble of thunder. Scattered misty raindrops began to fall, chilling the already crisp air. Arcturus halted to study the sky, wincing as a couple cold drops spattered on his eyelashes.

"The rain will come hard in a moment," he said gravely. "I don't think we'll find much shelter, so we'd best continue quickly."

He helped her over a muddy stretch, and soon they were running to stay ahead of the rain. Eventually, they were caught and ducked cautiously under the overhang of a lone boulder to wait it out. It was lacking in comfort, for only a little rain was kept out. They couldn't kneel for the mud.

Pleia shifted uncomfortably, trying not to lose her balance and fall against the spikes. Arcturus took her elbow to steady her and slid one of the three packs underneath her knees so she could rest.

"Thank you."

"You're welcome, my lady. Do you have a last name?"

Pleia rubbed her chilled hands together, recalling another cold day. . . the last day she had used that name.

"Aldebaran."

"It became fitting."

Pleia nodded.

Arcturus studied her face, then dropped a second pack for himself, after opening it and displaying a grain plait.

"Care for one? Highly nutritious on thorny runs."

He succeeded in bringing a smile to her face.

"Truly, but why not eat something that might not make them feel threatened? The thorns, I mean."

"I heartily agree."

He stowed the plait away and produced small loaves of travel bread, stuffed with wild potatoes, sweet herbs, and forester's cheese, the kind common in Tania and her sister villages. It was nutty, sweet, creamy and salty all at once, and there must have been some caffeine somewhere in the loaf, too, for both man and maiden were eager to set off in the lightening rain. Evening would not be far off.

Some time later, they stopped when, at their third wall, it became evident that they wouldn't find an easy way through anytime soon. Arcturus dropped the packs from his shoulders and rested them in his hands for a moment as he scanned the wall for a breach in thorns.

He glanced down when Pleia touched his wrist.

"Please, let me carry just one."

"My lady -"

"Pleia, please. You can't carry *everything*, Arc-" Her voice entreated as she looked up into his eyes. He stopped her.

"Just Arc."

"Please, Arc. Let me help you?"

Arc's eyes softened. He relented, removing heavier items from one satchel before he would give it to her.

That settled, they continued along the wall, Pleia happy to be carrying a share of her friend's load.

To their dismay, they could see no end to the thorns by the time the sun set, scalding the retreating storm clouds. Arcturus didn't say anything for a while as they continued on. There was no place to rest well here, and the feeling of the previous night was returning. The thorns were more alive than he had thought, and night was awakening them.

"Will you be alright for a little while more?"

Pleia nodded, though she was beginning to stumble. Those vines weren't helping any, and Arcturus was beginning to agree with her suspicions.

He sighed. "I don't trust those vines not to strangle us if we rest, Pleia. Tell me if you get too tired."

He put out his hand and cupped it under her elbow, ready to steady her when she stumbled again.

Pleia raised her eyes to her namesake and forced herself to keep going. They came to a breach topped by brambles; Arc drew his travel blade and, leaving Pleia, hacked the branches out of the way.

Pleia was exhausted. It would be another night without a dream of Maia; she was fearing that she was wasting everyone's time – she was staring at the thorns, too exhausted to tear her eyes away. She didn't notice that she was biting her lip until it bled, so deeply lost in thought as unbounded anxiety took her over until nothing else could break through.

Her hand snapped out and she instinctively reached for the thorns, for since her deep grief over her family, she had endured a bad habit of giving herself physical pain, to drain what was internal. She plunged her arm into the grasp of the briar. The thorns broke off, embedded in her arm.

Arcturus whirled at the odd, soft sigh as Pleia collapsed. Yet she struggled when the Guardian put his arms under her shoulders, lifting her from the ground.

"Pleia! No! Don't try to fight it. It's alright. You can't walk like this. Please, trust me to carry you."

His voice was reassuring.

Pleia tried to reply.

"Can't – everything. . ."

"I'm alright, Pleia. You're no burden for me to bear."

She gave up as he lifted her in his arms, bearing her up safely above the height of the brambles, and began to navigate the maze once more.

"I'll get those thorns removed once I have enough light. Need to find a place where I can build a fire without burning down the entire field," he muttered.

Indeed, save for the patches of swampy water, the area would be all too willing to burn. He began hunting for the well of which Trissa had spoken.

Pleia only murmured and gave a sigh in reply. Soon, her eyes closed.

VII
Anxiety

The moon was high and glinting off the cupola of the well when Arcturus broke out of the brambles. He sighed, for no one was there. He laid Pleia on the stone bench at the well's side and dropped the packs at last. He set about building a fire, and set out the warming stone, nearer to Pleia. It was lush enough here for flame due to the spring.

Soon the warmth and light of the fire was strong enough to see by. He stood for a few minutes as though he had neither walked nor borne a burden all day. His back was to the girl he was protecting.

The Pleiades were out again. Mysteriously, unyieldingly, always pointing northwest, no matter how the earth turned. Why did they seem to shine brighter than all the stars in the sky? And why did they shine second only to the star on Pleia's brow, whenever she removed the leather coronet? He wished she could lie there, quiet and at peace, until the stars faded again; let her not be anxious, not now.

As he was listening to the lone song of a nightingale, another sound cut through with the whish-wish of grass and branch being swept aside. A familiar voice was detailing some long trip years ago, when the well had been an easy landmark. Trissa and Dianthe appeared, trekking waist-deep through the grass, having happily followed the firelight.

"We're here, half a dozen mishaps later," Trissa called, spotting him. She stopped short as she realized not all of them were present. "Where's Eridan?"

"If he's not with you, he's on his own," Arcturus replied, moving to meet her. "Don't fear for him. He's a champion, after all, and even if he's fallen asleep, he'll have no trouble reaching us."

He brushed his sister's hair back with a comforting smile as she tried to look consoled.

"Come now, now that you're here, you must rest."

He followed Dia's glance to Pleia.

"She may have up to twenty thorns in her right arm and wrist. I have half a mind to wait until morning and let her sleep."

"Let her be," Trissa sighed, spreading her own blanket by the fire and curling up. "She could use a night where she doesn't have to blame herself for what she doesn't see. Now, you lie down, brother. There's no danger, and you're dead on your feet, if you can't already tell."

Arc was too weary to argue. He sat down with his back against the well and soon the night was quiet once more.

When morning came, a figure stole through the fog and into the camp.

Arc, no less awake, opened one eye as the intruder crouched beside Pleia, seeing the blood on her arm.

"About twenty thorns in her arm. You certainly took your time getting here. Don't tell me you got lost, now."

Eridan smiled at the laughing drawl.

"No less than you."

He rolled back Pleia's sleeve to inspect her forearm and wrist.

"I missed the well the first time and crossed to the end of the field before returning. I broke down a path from there to make it easier."

Arc got to his feet, buckling his vest and vambraces.

"You've had a long enough night. Why don't you rest while I free her?"

"I've done worse keeping watch of the Temple, though you might find that hard to believe," Eridan replied, laying aside the pack he had been carrying.

Between the two of them, the thorns were soon freed from Pleia's skin. A poultice of lamb's ear and yarrow, bound with some unwoven grasses from the plaits which Dianthe had made, soon wrapped Pleia's newly bleeding arm.

Pleia stirred, frowning a little at the sting of blood, and realized it was morning. She looked from one of her guardians to the other, torn between relief and apology.

"Morning, little Pleia," Eridan smiled. "You slept well, I hope?"

Still, she looked anxious.

"I am sorry," she said finally, especially to Arcturus.

"It's not your fault, Pleia."

"I shouldn't have put my arm in the bush," she murmured. "I felt useless. . . . I made myself even more so. I made you carry more than you ought when I meant to do otherwise."

Arc laid his hand on her bandaged wrist.

"Don't let yourself feel this way anymore, Pleia. You're not useless. I can always use a greater test, and that's all you gave me, not a burden. We wouldn't be following the Pleiades without you, and I assure you that Triss and I are grateful for the vacation."

Pleia smiled obediently then and began to pin up her tangled curls while the men moved to the fire to heat coffee.

Their approaching footsteps shocked Trissa out of a deep sleep and she shot upright, waking Dia. Both looked wildly about while Arc laughed and gave apology.

Triss' face lit up, looking at once like the child she had been before three tragedies ago.

"Eri!"

She flung her arms around him as he crouched.

"Good morning, little Tri," he chuckled.

"I was worried about you."

She looked plaintively into his eyes, unconcerned that her arms were still around his neck.

"I ended up on the other side of the field. It will be easier to get out now."

The relief in her face, and the smell of the coffee made him forget that he was tired. Dia managed to acquire a hug as Pleia appeared, looking scarcely worse for wear.

As soon as a wash had been had and the effects of caffeine were felt, the group began following the trail Eridan had blazed for them. This time, the women succeeded, happily, in lightening their guardians' loads.

As Trissa took the lead, Pleia found herself dropping back and walking beside Eridan as he brought up the rear.

"'Dan?"

Eridan turned at Pleia's hesitant voice.

"What is it, dearest?"

"I still . . . feel so useless."

He frowned.

"Whyever would you feel still feel useless?"

"I haven't dreamt of Maia in over a fortnight, and I fear it means this is all . . . only a dream, and I'm wasting your time, and Arcturus and Trissa's, and – everyone's hope."

She dropped her head, fighting the watering sensation in her eyes.

"I'm of no purpose on this trip as yet – we're only following the Pleiades, and look at me-"

She glanced at her wrist.

"I made myself a burden for Arc because of my anxiety."

Eridan put his arm around her.

"Pleia. . . even if you don't have a purpose now, it doesn't mean you won't have a role to play as time passes. It is Arc and Trissa who are the ones playing now: their purpose is to guide us safely, and mine is to protect you. But I don't even know why Dia is here, and neither does she. Your time will come, Pleia, as will hers. If it is of any comfort, regardless of the truth of the dream, without you and without it, I wouldn't have been able to reunite with my friends once more, and who knows what would have happened with the bears if we had not been there to delay their run. Trissa might not be here, the way she was feeling, Pleia. No one knows the worth of the small things they do. You're of great purpose, Pleia, even if you fear you don't have one."

They glanced up as a call came from the front-lines.

"Ha! I see ooopeeen fields!" Triss sang and sprinted ahead. Everyone followed suit.

At last, normal terrain – wildflowers in the vibrancy of fallen autumn leaves mingled with the soft haze of fairy bells. Dianthe began happily plucking blooms and weaving them, occasionally letting one fly on the breeze. Trissa twirled and inspected the northwesterly direction. Pleia would have liked to feel carefree for a moment, but only smiled at them both. As the Starbearer, her amusement had always been this way.

But one amusement she had always taken, freely – her song. She found herself whispering it beneath her breath, letting the wind softly stifle it before the men behind her could hear. She prayed as she never had that her dream was not the creation of her mind and of her fears.

> *"Speed the dawn, but may thy stars shine on,*
> *Be my hope in my breathless night.*
> *Remember, Morning Star, O Heaven's light,*
> *How thy Son is our Starbright!*
> *I'm only a nightingale singing in her plight*
> *Let your night cover me,*
> *Let your stars shine for me*
> *To you I give my heart, Queen of the Starry Sea*
> *Hear my plea,*
> *Your nightingale prays to thee!*
> *Cast a glance beyond the sea!"*

Scarcely had she finished when her eyes followed a songbird's flight; that was when all collectively realized that the sky above was no longer misted over. They were beyond the boundaries of old Celae – the sky was blue and clear, and brushed with cirrus clouds spun by wind.

Dia dropped to the ground in wonder, for she had little memory of that shade of blue. Pleia froze and stared upwards, acquiring a stiff neck for herself later on. Trissa drew a long gasp but was distracted, trying to pull Dianthe from the ground.

"Oooh, that looks familiar!" Eridan breathed.

Arcturus was helplessly torn between trying to help Triss with Dia, trying to keep Pleia from acquiring that neck ache while snapping her out of her awfully silent daydreams in which she wasn't breathing, and shouting – which he knew he shouldn't do because of potential foes potentially in hiding. Therefore, his gaze jerked from the women to the sky, back to the women, and then he joined Pleia in instantaneous exclamations about cloud shapes.

It took some amount of time for everyone to calm down enough to consider proceeding.

"I believe that we can reach the sea in twenty-four hours, if we make good time," Trissa declared, once Dianthe was able to stand without spinning dizzily. "I've never seen it, but Mother would always say how close it was. We seem to be constantly crossing

things, so with our luck, I hope we don't have to cross
the sea, too!"

Of course, they did.

VIII
Anomaly

It was not quite noon the following day when the group arrived at the coast of the sea of Adahara. A pristine, yet abandoned seaport lay in silence among the rolling waves.

Arcturus and Eridan proceeded slowly through the port, watching warily for enemies among its archways, columns, and westward-facing towers. It was truly empty, even of seacraft, and any human items which might be expected. A veranda looked over the quickly steepening shallows; a quay stretched out into the water, where the color was as deep as the sea's depths.

Trissa followed them without hesitation. Pleia had to stop Dianthe from darting down the veranda to inspect the shimmering of coral in the shallows, but soon Dia was made happy when Triss likewise jumped down in the sand. Eridan followed, still wary.

Pleia went to Arcturus' side where he stood on the quay.

The wind stirred the waves as they stood before it and the spray splashed them, playfully it seemed, and they both gasped, but not with the chill of the water: for the heart of a man will always be drawn over the sea, whence all is wonder.

Dia was busy investigating seashells, with which she soon filled her hands and pockets to overflowing. Trissa idly kicked driftwood, pretending she wasn't splashing in the water as she looked up and down the coastline. No boats or habitation were in sight.

Pleia stood with Arc on the quay. Arcturus gazed out over the ruffled waters; he noticed Pleia was looking up to him.

"What is it, Pleia?"

"Forgive me, it's only. . . I'm not used to being around men, before this journey, except for Eridan and for the Temple Fathers and acolytes, and they're so. . . quiet. You're different. Not so much, I suppose. I'm sorry, I don't mean to make you feel -"

"No, it's alright. Do I frighten you?"

"It's not you. . . I am frightened but I assume the best of your kind. And also the worst, after all those years ago."

"Pleia. I will never, ever, hurt you. As Eridan says, I will do my best by you that I can. You don't need to be afraid of me."

Pleia's eyes searched his and then softened.

"I know."

She dropped her gaze and let him take her arm. They turned their minds to the question at hand.

"I don't see a way to cross, if we must," Pleia murmured.

"Well, we could construct a ship of some kind, but it might take a fortnight, at least, to make her truly seaworthy."

"What's across the sea? Do you know? I was never taught much geography beyond the bounds of Celae."

"Nothing much to my knowledge. Halfway out past the stretch of Adar, there used to be inhabited land, but it's all washed away now, and 'tis only open ocean."

"A city, maybe?"

"I suppose there might have been. You think of the legend."

Pleia bit her lip.

"It would make sense. If it was sunken and did hold a promise to that which Antaré broke, it would give us something to look for, if we had the means."

"We'll find the means, or be given them. Don't worry."

"What if. . . it was only a dream?"

"Still worried? Then never mind, for you've aided the kingdom by us Guardians, if nothing else comes of it."

He touched the band on her brow.

"And I wouldn't trade the journey, Pleia, for anything."

Neither saw the slimy, slender tentacle that slithered silently from the water over the stone and curled around Pleia's ankle. She didn't feel it until she was dragged into the water.

"Pleia!"

When her head didn't appear a moment after, Arc frantically tore off his leather jerkin and dove in after her. Eridan and the others came running.

"'Dan, he can't hold his breath this long!" Trissa gasped, when several minutes had passed with no sign of man or maiden.

"Stay! I'll find them!" Eridan flung his swordbelt aside and was about to plunge in when Arc's head broke the surface. Pleia bobbed up beside him, clinging to his arm as she coughed.

Arc shook his hair out of his eyes.

"Now who's taking their time?" Eridan scolded in relief, jumping down the step.

"Weirdest thing I've seen, indubitably," Arc panted, treading water. "Twenty feet of ocean and then twenty feet of falling through the air for a decent dose of bruises. What nabbed Pleia was only some ferocious seaweed with a mind of its own."

Dia cocked her head in confusion.

"I second whatever you're thinking," Trissa blinked.

"He wasn't helped by the fact that I can't swim," Pleia moaned, half laughing as she struggled, giving Arc a grateful glance as he continued to support her and drew her closer to the step.

"I should have taught you a long time ago," Eridan sighed, fishing Pleia out. She sat on the step and leaned her head on him.

Dia was still asking silent questions.

"Climbed until we reached the water, easy enough," Arc supplied, taking a seat beside Pleia. "However. . . not sitting this close to the water might be wise for you, Pleia, because you're a trip-hazard, or at least, that star's aura seems to attract them."

"The truth of that statement cannot be under-stated," Eridan drawled. "Things are always viciously tripping her ever since we left the Temple, weirdly enough. I think they're out to get you, dear, or at least the earth is. They may well be trying to wipe the star from your brow, but none of us will let you fall, I promise."

They all scooted up to the veranda's deck.

"So," Arc began, fishing a waterlogged Constellarium from the pouch at his waist. "We could take the route of proceeding under the sea, since there's air to breathe, and this device – if it still works -" he gave it a shake. "-Will help us stay on track since we won't be able to see the stars."

Trissa contemplated the notion for a moment.

"I'm just wondering. What happens if a shark falls out of the sea like you did, and falls on top of us?"

"Then we punch it in the nose," Eridan offered.

"It's too cold this season for sharks."

"Do you truly know anything about sharks, Arc?"

"No, except that they have teeth and besides, if one falls out of the sea it will be too busy hyperventilating and figuring out its predicament to try and eat you. Unless it happens to inhale you in so doing, and then you're rather out of luck unless its teeth miss you on the way in."

"Arc - sometimes, you're not particularly comforting to us three."

Trissa pulled Dia's arm around her and gave her a hug.

"I'm teasing, I had to fight the air bubble to get through to Pleia," Arc smiled. "No sharks will rain down. However, I'm beginning to doubt that the Constellarium will prove of use. I wish I had remembered it was in my pocket."

"I'd rather it drown than Pleia," Eridan said gently. "We'll be alright without it, but I think that negates the confusion of the seafloor. Still. . . Pleia, what was it that Maia said to you in your dream?"

"She said to call her, and she would be here."

"Maybe try that song you've always sung to her, in all your times of trouble," he suggested. "The one you always asked me to give a drone for, to stand-in for the song of the Starpool."

Pleia looked nervously at the spreading ocean. If no answer came-!

Her guardian squeezed her hand.

"I don't doubt she'll answer you," he whispered, and his eyes promised that he trusted her. He dropped a glance back at the other three, who were listening with interest. "It's alright, I'll drone for you; don't worry."

Pleia took a deep breath, nodding. Eridan began to hum the shimmering note which Pleia had heard emanating from the Starpool. She had stanzas for everything, she thought with a little sigh, and began to sing,

> *"Gentle lady of the stars,*
> *You drew me here through many scars;*
> *Mother of the starry skies,*
> *Your voice has called me to your side!*
> *Hear my plea,*
> *O Sweetest Queen,*
> *Who bound the star upon my brow,*
> *Your light a gift,*
> *Grant it now!*
> *Lady of Hope!*
> *Smile on me*
> *O Maia, I turn to thee,*
> *Protect me, Mother of the Starry Sea!*
> *Hear my plea,*
> *Help us in our need*
> *Part the waters,*
> *Brighten the shade*
> *Glorious Queen,*
> *Hear and answer me!"*

For a minute, there was nothing new of note; Pleia almost hung her head and turned away, when Eridan grasped her arm. Two streaks of foam were funneling towards them from the distance with an increasing hum. The waves began to ripple silverine like fishscale; the streaks wove across each other and slammed into the end of the pier where Pleia and Eridan stood. A wave crashed upwards and Pleia was hard-pressed not to laugh and gasp at the same time, as both she and her companion were thoroughly soaked by seawater.

When they raised their eyes, trying to keep water from dripping into them, all was still once more.

"No, please," Pleia pleaded softly, looking for any further signs.

"Hush," Eridan said, for something was rumbling through the quay beneath their feet.

The water surged in foam and spray, shedding like fountain tears as monolithic stones like honeycomb erupted to the surface, and coral and anemones were wiped away. Stone after stone settled and locked, rising one after another, until a pathway stretched as far as the eye could see across the waves.

"Oh oh oh!" and Pleia sighed in delight as her heart seemed to rush with the water. "She did – it is – oh, oh, 'Dan!'"

Eridan began laughing softly and gave her a decidedly drenched embrace.

"I told you, you were a silly sweetheart for questioning yourself. One doesn't simply have a dream for seventeen years for no reason, pumpkin."

Trissa was shrieking gleefully in the background, narrowly keeping Dia from throwing handfuls of shells in the air, whilst Arc barely managed to keep them both on dry land. He grinned at Pleia as though he, too, were seconding Eridan's words.

"Come now, Pleia, you're still drenched, and before we do aught else you need to change," Eridan commanded.

He sent her to the building at the end of the veranda, which Arc gave a quick scout of. The Guardian left her to exchange her shaded cerulean travel robe for one of seafoam hue, marked with the Temple's seven colored stones.

"There you are! Dia thinks we shall have to travel quickly, and I agree, for I suppose there's not much shelter on this bridge when night falls," Trissa called over her shoulder, darting off across the stones as both men jumped after her.

"Well, I guess we're going!" Arc shrugged, and off they went. The quiet burbling of the sea which followed them came with the sinking of each stone as they passed over, leaving the sea innocently unabridged.

Contrary to assumptions, after an uneventful walk, the group came to a pavilion which seemed designed as a resting place. The benches along the openly latticed walls were cushioned with a thick, velvety moss; a room off to the side served for washing, for there was an inexplicable pool of fresh water.

"This can't have been magically – I mean, miraculously built for us, could it?" Trissa inquired, dubiously fingering the remains of a seasilk curtain.

"It appears to have been a road, judging by its unnecessary width, and I believe I'm seeing wagon treads worn into the stone," her brother replied, gladly dropping his load. He laid out the warming stones for some light.

"A road built to pop out of the ocean that has only been this far inland for. . . maybe a couple centuries," Eridan mused.

"The sea may have been inland before," Pleia suggested, taking up a bench at his behest. She began to grind the plaited grains for flatbread.

"That's all I can think of," Arc agreed. "At any rate, it leads somewhere, and I feel we'll find the city, Pleia."

The rest of the evening fell into the weaving of restless tales among the baking and breaking of bread; the sun sank its glowing heart into the sea.

IX

Clarity

Pleia opened her eyes to a fresh ocean breeze and something cold lying against her hand. The sun was just beginning to rise and paint the sky rose and mauve. For a moment, she lay there, thinking she was asleep, dreaming of the ruffling of a sail and the ocean.

Then she glanced down and saw that something wrapped in rubbery silver skin lay at her feet, its head beneath her hand. She jumped, and it did likewise, black orb-like eyes staring at her anxiously. Pleia laughed and touched the seal's nose.

"Good morning, little one! What are you doing? Did you come to see the sunrise?"

She swung her legs over the bench, speaking quietly, for the others were still asleep. The seal flopped along after her as she slipped from the pavilion and curled up on the western pathway. She prayed before the sunrise, as she had been wont to do every morning at the Temple. The seal rested its head in her lap.

81

Once Pleia had finished, her companion hopped into the water, splashing her and making her giggle. Pleia wiped seawater from her face and splashed him back.

"Pleia?" Arc ducked from the pavilion, drawing on his coat. He smiled slowly, taking in the scene. "What are you up to? Recall what I told you about being near the edge?"

He burst out laughing at the mournful expression on both faces and dropped down beside Pleia.

"Never mind, I'll keep an eye out for bloodthirsty seaweed."

He took her arm, examining the skin as he lifted the bandages.

"Looks like these can come off now. How do you feel?"

"It ceased its stinging last evening. The thorns must have been in deep, for it to last so long."

"Yes, and they hold a great deal of poison; I'm surprised you haven't been so weary."

He removed the lamb's ear wrap and threw it in the water, where the seal took it up for play.

"I think the blue sky helped," Pleia smiled, drinking in the shifting colors of the sky.

"Mm, and maybe that star purges poison."

Pleia glanced at Arc as he studied her gravely, only to be interrupted by the awakening of the rest of the party.

"Dia demands to know, 'what on earth is that?' She thinks it's a shark," Trissa's voice floated down to them.

Dia had evidently jerked her up from sleep and was pointing to the creature; the latter had settled for a banana-like pose on the edge of the road.

"This little fellow?" He's a seal, not a shark! At least, I think he is, though he doesn't quite look like the drawings of the Temple books."

"Sharks have sharp teeth and mean faces, I promise. They don't look like bananas!" was Arc's addition. "Though, does he look anything like a dinosaur, Pleia?"

Pleia looked down at the creature. "Hm, judging by the varied odd illustrations, he might be."

She placed one fingertip on the seal's head so it glanced up at her.

"You're not a meat-eating dinosaur, are you?"

Both she and the seal nodded at the same time.

"He's a meat-eating dinosaur, Dia, that wants cuddles," she announced.

The seal arfed happily and began flopping towards the pavilion as fast as his flippers could carry him.

Eridan, having been silently awake the whole time, could be heard laughing from his bench as Dianthe tried to hide behind Trissa, to no avail.

But there was little time to be spent thus, and soon they were walking; the pavilion disappeared into the waves.

They walked for hours until the eyes ached at the solitary sight of sea.

"I was wondering-" Pleia began, and stopped.

"Wondering what?" Eridan asked, trying not to yawn.

"The boat. I didn't think we wouldn't see it."

Sure enough, as they drew closer, the road dropped away. A pearlescent sloop stood at the ready.

Dianthe gave a sound that was almost a whimper.

"We'll get there soon." Pleia touched the maid's shoulder. "I know, we're all tired of the journey. It didn't take so long in my dream."

The boat rocked as they stepped into it and cast off.

Night fell; it was the first of many. The moon passed silently overhead, followed swiftly by the sun;

but ever the waves drew them on, and a steady wind filled the white sail with its star and bore them northwest.

Pleia looked down through the water; sometimes when the sun was shining, the waves were as clear as glass, and she saw glimpses of ruined hillsides strewn with ancient homes destroyed in that long-ago flood. Sometimes, they didn't seem damaged at all, eerily, as though they were still filled by breath.

Arcturus stood, handling the sail with Eridan, breathing in the salty air with delight. Trissa spent her time either at the tiller, playing her flute, or up in the rigging to feel the wind on her face, vexing her brother.

The closer they came, the more they wondered what they might face: if it might, oh sweet rest, be only a simple, healing stop, and some relic, perhaps. But they all feared it was too easy a dream, and their souls were already aching for home.

"I don't suppose this could end easily," Trissa faltered. She was leaning on Eridan's shoulder.

"The island was peaceful. I feel it will be easy for you. I think you need not worry."

Pleia's eyes were fastened on an odd wall of mist on the horizon. The straggling arms of the lands of Rada and Adar were falling back in the distance.

Eridan shifted uncomfortably at her words, stopping Trissa as she moved to rise. Arc, too, seemed ill at ease, and came beside Pleia to watch the fog.

"There's no reason for fog there, not at this time," he mused, after a moment of resting his hand on her shoulder.

"Must be our destination, then," Eridan surmised.

"The distance seems right." Pleia touched Arc's hand lightly in thanks.

Sure enough, the boat sent itself into the mist. There was always mist these days, it seemed. This one was so dense and creamy that even the waves at the ship's sides were obscured.

"Dia?" Pleia turned at something she thought she heard. "Do you hear anything?"

Her friend listened as the others sat still. Dianthe nodded slowly and with a peculiar look, tapped her feet on the deck.

Footsteps.

From whence? Pleia could neither sense nor see solid ground nearby.

Arc shifted a lock on the spiked vambraces, the almost imperceptible click sounding like the crack of a whip. Eridan and Trissa's hands hovered at their weapons' grips.

The ship bumped and bobbed softly as though it had been taken hold of; swifter, swifter it was drawn, until the wave crests flung up and over the passengers; yet the water was oddly warm, and the ache began to leave their limbs. Dianthe began laughing, enjoying the ride as the prow tilted upwards against the waves.

As instantly as it had sped, it slowed. The fog broke with a gleam of sunlight that turned it into a wall of diamonds.

There lay the pier, just as Pleia had described, only now there was a lush, sea-salted moss which draped it like flowering vines.

But it was less than the man who stood upon the pier, silver line in hand, which was bound to the ship's bow, and which vanished when the craft came to lie still in the water.

The only word to describe him was angelic; he stood still, eyes lowered upon Pleia, the ghost of a smile playing over his lips and dashing through his eyes. An opal star glimmered high on his brow among crested waves of platinum.

Pleia held her breath, gazing into his face. She started to move to meet him, gently brushing Arcturus' hand aside as he held her back. The maiden came slowly under the stranger's gaze, just before him. Only then did he stir, and his eyes glowed with laughter as he smiled.

"It has taken you a long time, little one."

Pleia gasped softly and ducked into his arms as her companions slowly disembarked the ship.

"Yours was one of the faces I thought I could see," Pleia remembered, meeting his gaze timidly.

"Yes, I and my brothers; and souls whose freedom only you can gain. My brothers we shall meet; the others, your soul will find alone."

He nodded to her companions.

"I am Ireo, keeper of the city, one of the three set in stone. I was sent to draw you from the waters, within which is much darkness. I cannot take you far, only to the field; there you may rest, until Pleia has been sent for."

"Maia?" Pleia hesitated.

"I can say naught about what lies before you, for many things are hidden by the mist of Scier. But I have come to warn you, Pleia: should you enter here, you will be broken. For only the broken souls may shine with starlight."

He looked at her sorrowfully, speaking quietly so that she alone could hear.

Yet Pleia knew. She had always known it wouldn't be so simple as in her dream. If it had been. . . why dream for seventeen years? Nothing worth gaining could be had without a fight.

She nodded, and with a little smile, he took her hand and led them all into the field.

"You will see me anon, little one. I will not say goodbye."

He dissipated into the sheer mist.

Pleia gazed upon the vale and felt that she was dreaming. She reached for the wet grass, as damp as it had been; it didn't cling to her fingers, and the little blooms bent with every brush of breeze.

"I don't understand," Pleia heard herself whisper, and Eridan did, too.

"Understand what, little one?" He didn't seem surprised.

"A-Anything. Maia told me that 'This is a place which once was mine, and that of Scier, but it was taken away and plunged into a darkness which will soon cover your world.' But if that is true, why is Ireo here? Why? Why anything? What is this place? I don't know why it needs me, why it needs us."

She had noted the barely visible sliver of moon hanging in the sky; if the legends were true, they were running out of time. But there was always enough time, wasn't there?

She watched as Trissa flung her cloak on the dew-bedecked ground and curled up, dreamily studying the cloudy, starry sky overhead.

"I'm so confused, 'Dan, I feel like I'm asleep, and that frightens me."

"Mm, in some ways that might be better than waking up to reality," he laughed softly, "yet I swear, Pleia, you're as awake as I am."

He squeezed her hand.

"I think we'll find all the answers here. For now, let's do as Ireo says, and rest while we wait. Heaven knows, Pleia, that you haven't been sleeping well! So do me a favor and sleep now."

He set her down among the flowers and wouldn't depart until she closed her eyes. Then he took himself to the other side of the vale, where he dropped down to talk to Arc; the latter was lying on his back with his legs crossed over a stone, idly weaving the long grass with one hand; Dianthe and Trissa had already fallen asleep.

Pleia didn't sleep.

You will be broken.

She thought of what could lie before her. What could break her, far beyond fear and pain? Her eyes kept being drawn to her companions and a chill would run through her soul.

No. They could not be broken, too.

She sighed and closed her eyes.

A sound was growing in her ears, one she hadn't heard over the waves, and one of which she had dreamed.

Honey, waterfalls, and bells! It was drawing her heart, she couldn't resist – she opened her eyes once more. The others were all resting.

Let them stay safe, Ireo, she prayed, and rising, began to fly towards the sound.

Something snapped Arc's eyes open with a scowl and he checked on the others. All was well, except that Pleia was halfway out of sight.

"Oh, Pleia!" he muttered, and struck Eridan's arm. "Stay with Trissa and Dia! I'm going with the Star-Bound. It would seem she's been summoned."

With that, he ran through the mist.

X

Archenemy

"Pleia? Pleia, answer me!" Arc's voice rang back into his ears as it bounced off the ancient, terraced walls he had entered. Here the mist hid most from sight. This wasn't the city, but a palisade where guards might have watched the sea and the stranded quay.

He moved slowly, every now and then as his senses picked up faint sounds and airs of a presence, but no one was there, and Pleia did not answer. If Ireo was present, the island was surely safe – was that reasonable to believe? Something in his mind said no as he struggled not to chide himself for following, and he pressed onward.

Down the stairs and through empty archways, he came upon a raised courtyard, balconied on all sides. The soft sea breeze refreshed the air among ancient blooms.

"Pleia!"

She turned from looking out toward the barely visible blue of the sea. Her face lit up.

"Arc!" She came and stopped before him, smiling shyly.

"Pleia, didn't you hear me calling? Why did you run?"

She dropped her head.

"Forgive me, I didn't hear you. I had to go; I couldn't wait." She tilted her head back again and smiled, saying simply, "I wanted you to rest. I'm so happy that you came here with me. . . so you could see it."

Arcturus found himself gazing down at her, melting at everything she said. It was as though Pleia was a child again, innocent, and held safe by memory.

"I've never seen you happy, truly, have I."

"No . . . I've always been afraid. But here . . . just for a moment, I feel I am with Maia, that everything is well, will be well . . . I remember her so clearly now."

She closed her eyes as though the breeze was the kiss Maia had left upon her forehead, but something passed over her face like a shadow.

"I was scared you'd get hurt if you came." She bit her lip and Arc saw the blood appear. "I was afraid! afraid," she breathed, a tear trickling down her cheek. "Ireo said I'd be broken, and what can break me but that – I'll lose you, all of you-" She looked up into his eyes. "And I'll be alone again. . . I can't! I can't, I want to protect you, won't you let me?"

"Oh Pleia. . ." He took her hands and held them safely. "You need to let me protect you, but if I need saving and it won't cost you, I won't argue. Now, Deo knows you better and so there may be something else that breaks you," he reminded her. "He knows what you need. We're not lost yet."

Pleia nodded and looked up again. "Isn't it pretty?" she sighed, turning his eyes over the misty vale. "I'd never been here before. I didn't see much in the mist. I should have gone straight ahead, but I was confused when I saw this place. It feels like a dream!"

She faltered.

"It isn't, is it? You're not a dream, are you?"

"This isn't a dream, Pleia. Verily, if it is, I'm having the same one."

He managed to draw a little smile back to her lips.

"You won't go away?"

"Not if I don't have to."

She smiled happily and turned her head away.

Abruptly, she murmured timidly but adorably, "Which of your ribs is missing?"

Arc stopped and eyed her in amusement.

"What did they teach you at the Temple?"

Pleia stared at him, anxious.

"Was that wrong to ask?"

Arc started, then stopped.

"No, it's not; but, anatomically-" He stopped again, helplessly, looking at her. Internally, he sighed. "Right side."

Pleia's face lit up and she jumped to his right side and hugged him hard.

"You'll. . . come back with me?"

Arc's brow creased a little. "You never said. . . whether you have to go back to the Temple?"

"I'm not consecrated, not like the others. Well. . . I suppose the star is a consecration." She was troubled now.

"It'll work out, Pleia, any way it goes. I'll go back with you, and we will find out. Eridan is in charge of you, isn't he?"

Pleia's eyes lit up again. "Yes, I suppose he's the only one over me. I was never under the fathers, except as they are priests."

Arc grinned. "And I hardly think Eridan is going to argue."

"Maybe," Pleia said cheerfully, pulling at the star clasping his cloak. "Thank you for coming, I'd be. . .anxious, alone. There's something I now feel that is foreboding, more than the hallucinations, that I never felt then."

"That's because you're so concerned you're a nightmare," he teased, lightly.

"Either me, or I'm having one of you," she sighed.

"Well, again, if I'm a nightmare, I'm having a dream," he replied, almost serious as he laid his hand on the star, and she exhaled with the distant ocean waves.

"Where were you going, Princess? Shall we go?"

"I was following the sound of the Starpool," she replied. "It's all I can think of, since that's all Maia showed me."

"Then off we go," Arc declared, and taking hold of her arm lest she run off once more, they proceeded down into the field.

Pleia kept glancing back.

"I feel someone is following us," she confided.

"I had the same feeling, but didn't want to worry you," Arc returned, not turning his eyes aside.

"Perhaps it's Dianthe – she tends to follow me."

"Mm."

But Arc didn't offer an agreement. He knew that Dianthe had been soundly asleep when he had left the meadow.

The vale sloped downwards; an alabaster city rose above them, and now when Pleia looked to the sky, the stars were glittering like the dust of diamonds. Fireflies glowed softly, resting on the petals of the wildflowers there, the rosy dianthus and violet primrose.

A lake pooled at their feet like liquid opal, leaving a pathway identical to the ocean road. The city stood, alyssum-white despite the moss adorning its crests and the hovering, olive-tinged clouds at every parapet. It might have been carved of pearl, so surreal was it. The southeastern lake was shallow, almost freshwater due to a plentitude of springs; in the northwest, the city was surrounded on three sides by seawater, as the bay spread out into open sea.

Pleia gave a little sigh, trying not to be distracted by the pink flowers blooming beneath the water and the tiny teal minnows. Even from where she stood, she could see, high up, a familiar courtyard. She started off down the path with her heart trying not to beat to every second she had left.

The nearer they drew, the better they could see that dark, strangling vines of thorn were struggling up the lower walls like a net striving to keep the city silent.

The entry was a wide gateway, crowned by three broken marble figures, which might have been angels in starry robes.

The city was still yet felt alive, but the streets were as empty as they had always been. Still lay the remnants of city life: a broken doll, an open door, pitchers at the fountain.

Chills ran up Pleia's arms, and she rubbed them to cure the goosebumps. As she turned her head, almost-faces faded in and out of view. Some, perhaps, were Ireo's brothers; she remembered those smiling glances from long ago, but all others felt steeped in sorrow. Pleia shut her eyes and prayed, wishing she had thought to pray before, hoping she could find the way for them.

Arc seemed to see them, too. He fell silent, looking at the porcelain doll lying broken at his feet. He found, before Pleia did, signs of war. Smoke-scalded stones, broken blades. All else had faded away.

Whoever had been here – whatever the day had been – the tragedy was about to repeat itself in Celae. Arc tightened his lips and his grip on Pleia's arm.

The sound of the Starpool was floating down from somewhere high above.

"This way," Pleia whispered, and drew Arc up a winding road. It spiraled upwards like a shell, and soon brought them out to a breathing space, an overlook thinly sheltered by a shallow cistern. It was marked into four rectangles, with a cross-walkway through the water, and in the center was erected a bronze pedestal.

A greenish cloud was curling at the cistern's edge, where it dropped off to the streets far below. Slender, sculpted columns rose like trees from the shallow pool, painted and carved in relief. The images fascinated Pleia, and she hung back as Arc stepped to the edge.

From there, the mist was transparent enough to see beyond the lake, into the meadow and out to sea. Arc strained to see whether the others remained at rest, but he could not see. He waved the green fog away with a frown, but Pleia had no interest in the view. She held out her hand and he returned.

"These pillars. . . they're like a history book." Pleia turned Arc's gaze upwards to the image of the city being erected. Where they were standing, they were in the middle of the account.

"Let's backtrack," Arc proposed, now equally fastened upon the prospect of unraveling the mystery.

The pillars soon proved to be read, not round about the column, but the western side across the row to the north, until the row was broken by the path; and then down one row to the East, proceeding south. Each of the four quadrants spoke of a different age of the city.

The northeastern spoke of ancient times; Alultaurari had been founded upon a hill through which great cracks ran, from the earthquake at Scier's death, and where lay a strange pool, which came to be known as the Starpool. In previously pagan times, it had been sacred for its power of magnifying the stars, even in daytime, and had been a pilgrimage site.

To the south, they learned of the coming of Scier's light to the kingdom. Once Christianity had spread, Alultaurari grew from a tiny village into the ancient royal city, due to its love and devotion to Scier and His Mother. Alultaurari's patronage was that of the archangels, for in age-old legend, it was they who had driven the cracks through the earth, driving the demons deep down within, and created the Starpool to cleanse the land with its pure mirroring of heaven's light.

And then came a story which gave Pleia chills, and with every step, she heard the voiceless whispering of souls pressing in on her. She gripped Arc's wrist to keep her sanity and he in turn kept her rigidly at his side.

The city gradually encompassed surrounding lands until it became a great kingdom. The prophecy and kingship were given to the mute shepherd, Dà-El, when he became the first to defend Scier and Maia against the spreading heresies; a king had been sought for, and after a vision of Scier, the boy had come and laid his hand over the Starpool, and the King's star, Regulus, had shone brightly.

"Wait," Pleia breathed, touching the carving before her eyes. "Dà-El . . . he was the first king of Celae. He's one of Dianthe's ancestors. She said that he was the tamer of the wild beasts from the beginning, before the founding of Celae."

Indeed, as in the formal image before them, Dà-El was forever depicted with bears and great cats, and a strange sea creature termed monstrous.

The carvings called it *Pleisiasaurus Morsquasitor*, the death-seeker. Seven bioluminescent patches on its head resemble the Pleiades; and a regal frill framed its sharply toothed skull.

It had terrorized the shore, and any ships sailing out, until Dà-El had dared to ride it, dropping from a ship's mast, and with his courage and gentleness, tamed it, naming it Ahknett-Minazal. It had then become friend, such that the lower levels of the city were carved out into a home for it, where the people could watch her dance through the water, and she became a protector at sea, where she had once been enemy.

The story continued, shifting focus to Dà-El's kingdom guardian, Tauré -

"-Aldebaran," Arc read aloud. "Then. . . he must be your ancestor, Pleia. To think your ancestors were friends, as you and Dia are. And look!"

He marked the carving with his finger, for there was depicted Tauré's daughter, Gienna, and upon her brow was the same star-scar. She was the kingdom's shepherdess, the first recorded Star-bright, and Dà-El's love.

"Again?" Pleia whispered, searching the image with her eyes. "I thought there was only one before me, Rána."

The carvings continued, introducing yet another set of ancestors, this time the forerunners of the modern tribe of the Guardians. Known as the Tureis, they, too, had initially been outsiders, wandering men in tune with the Earth. They were brought into the kingdom when there was trouble with a northern tribe and poisoned deer, and the Star-Bright enlisted their aid.

Arc and Pleia stopped. The next pillar had been started, but the image was only half-formed, half-sketched, and broken.

The entire northwestern quadrant was empty.

"What happened?" Arc muttered. "This hasn't cleared up much. There must be a written log somewhere, where they had a little more to put down. Unless it was completely sudden."

"Perhaps in the palace or cathedral?"

"Left you on a cliffhanger, has it?"

A low laugh sounded behind them and Pleia jumped.

The pair spun around to face a dark-toned man in poorly-matched charcoal and bronze. He leaned on an uncarven column, idly fingering a few ancient coins he had dredged from the cistern.

"Uhh. . . Antaré?" Arc instinctively pulled Pleia close to him so that she was sheltered by his shoulder.

"Antaré?" the girl breathed. "How could it be? He can't have made it through – this makes no sense!"

"You're right," Arc whispered back, hand sliding towards the lock on his arm. "Unless, he's a hallucination or dark matter."

"Arc!" Pleia hissed, stopping his hand. "Remember, you only have one shot with either of your weapons. We're better off getting away, regardless of whether he's physical or not."

Arc relaxed but eyed the laughing Antaré guardedly.

"Then let's see what this cloud of dust has to say, shall we?"

"You're wondering why I'm here."

"How, more precisely."

Antaré shrugged, dropping the coins into his pocket and languidly moving around the pedestal.

"I have my ways."

"That's a generic cover if I ever heard one," Arc said, aside.

Pleia's eyes didn't leave Antaré, recoiling as he drew closer.

Antaré stopped at the barely begun pillar and surveyed it.

"Dying to know, aren't you. Well, I'll spare you." His eyes gleamed and his teeth seemed fanged like a snake's. "You'd wonder how I know – oh yes, my ancestor lived here. Mm-hm, fine, average fellow. Only, he's dead, ancient history, you might say."

He laughed again and gave the column a kick, flaking loose pieces from the carving's edges.

"That Dà-El, he was chosen to step down. Of course, he refused, caused a rebellion within the city; my ancestor took the helm and did his best, but that Dà-El."

Antaré shook his head.

"Caused the poison leak, the town went mad, the bears went mad, everything went mad – yes, that's it: disaster, disaster for them and now this far down the line, his fault usurped *my* throne, so I'm here to get it back."

His eyes narrowed.

"And so are you. You, trying to take *my* throne – to make Celae fall so you can rule!"

His lips twisted.

"No one makes Celae fall but me. For all the times the Temple Guardian thwarted my decision to remove you and your dangers from our kingdom, Princess, he's going to wish he'd let me, isn't he? How could you let them think you were helping them save Celae?"

"You and I both know there's no antidote to the poison here, just as well as we know Maia never called you, and never placed that mark on your brow. But you never let anyone see it wash off, do you? Yet when the Starpool sees that gem. . . oh yes, that's what will release the poison. That's what Gienna did for Dà-El, all those years ago. And don't think Rána did any better. Those beasts were known to be well before she touched them. You'll be the crowning jewel, won't you?"

"Enough!" Arc said sharply. "Your serpent's tongue is twisted in knots."

His hand gently cupped over Pleia's hair. She was staring at Antaré, wordlessly wide-eyed in horror.

"What did she offer you, Guardian? Half the throne? I may have exiled you, but I'm surprised! It's only the oldest trick in the book!"

Arc's eyes narrowed to match Antaré's.

"Not quite. There's one older, and you failed miserably."

Arc's hand moved to the lock on his arm as Antaré tensed.

Antaré's lip curled. He struck out as Arc side-stepped and pushed Pleia behind the nearest column.

Arc blocked a second blow with his spear, twisting Antaré's arm back, slamming the back of his wrist against the edge of the pedestal. The knife fell – but Antaré kicked a wave of the green mist into Arc's face. The spear clattered to the ground.

"Arc!"

He was grasping his head as though something were trying to rip free, and his shoulders were shaking as his muscles rebelled.

"Arc!"

Antaré sneered at her and stepped around the Guardian, but Pleia's voice cut through whatever Arc was feeling and he looked at her, grimacing and shaking as though a lightning-rent fence wrapped him round.

It was the poison. Why she hadn't noticed it creeping after them before, she didn't know.

Maybe that star purges poison -

"Arc, Arc! Stay! Don't let go!" She fixed her eyes on his as Antaré reached her side. She almost didn't notice as he slammed her back into the cistern and held her face firmly beneath the eight inches of water.

"ANTARÉ!"

Arc lunged into the cistern and ripped Antaré's hands from Pleia's shoulders.

"Just try to run me through," Antaré whispered, cackling and unconcerned as Arc pinned him against the column. "I may slip through your fingers. . . and be behind you."

No sooner said than done.

Arc whirled, seizing Pleia's hand, and dragged her away through the stone forest.

XI

Ancestry

Darting through and around the pillars offered little stealth if they slipped from the raised stones. Arc pulled Pleia through and about the ruined walls of a home and set her in a sheltered corner.

"You stay here," he directed. "I'll draw him, or it, away and then I'll return."

"But – if it's only a hallucination or dark matter," Pleia began to object.

He put a finger to his lips.

"I can't take that chance, Pleia. I need to make sure you're safe, so I won't be gone long."

He sprinted out the way they had come. Pleia's eyes followed him through the window, feeling as though she had swallowed a heavy stone. Her fingers unfeelingly touched the star on her brow. She knew Antaré had spoken falsely, but he had been so convincing –

Arc didn't seem to believe any of it. But the rest of the story must be equally false –

And yet, that stone was still sinking. She clung to the hope that Arc didn't doubt her and that Antaré was only an all-too vivid hallucination and couldn't hurt him.

And that the poison wouldn't find him while she wasn't there.

She waited impatiently for Arc to return, listening to every faint crunch of gravel.

"That didn't last long, did it?" a voice surmised, jerking Pleia's gaze from the window. She scrambled to her feet.

Antaré was leaning against the crumbling wall, inspecting a bronzed orb from a curtain tassel. Discarding it, he glanced at the maiden.

"Now, you really want to rethink this, don't you, Princess?"

He advanced.

Ghost or cloud of dust, Pleia had no level of frustration left on which to back away. She threw herself forward, plunging through the image, her foot catching on a loose stone as she tripped to a halt.

She raised her confused eyes to meet Arc's equally quizzical gaze as he paused in the doorway.

"What are you doing?"

Pleia stared a moment and shook her head to clear her confusion.

"An-Antaré. I didn't want to wait to find out if he were real, and it would confuse him, so I ran through him."

Arc raised an eyebrow with a half smile.

"Um. . .alright, but don't repeat that if there's a next time. Nice way to get straight to the point, though. So much for me 'drawing him away,' so I'm glad you're alright. Now, let's find the log and the Starpool, shall we?"

He offered her his hand but noticed she was still perturbed.

"What is it, little maid?"

"You. . . you still believe me, then?"

His eyes softened.

"My dear Pleia. Would I sooner believe a soulless cloud of dust than you? You've had your chances to disprove yourself, if only by inconsistencies, and you haven't."

"Can I prove it?"

"I don't need you to."

"I know, but *I* need to!" Pleia faltered, nervously beginning to rub the scar as though to wipe it away.

"Pleia."

Arc caught her hands and pulled them away from her face, stooping.

"I need you to love yourself enough to trust yourself to trust me that I love you, and so I trust you."

She studied his face as that sank in, rewarding him with the child Pleia's smile.

"I trust you."

She accepted his hand, and he guided her outside. Caution had become their best friend; they slipped from doorway to doorway.

"What if he was right?" she wondered aloud.

For the hundredth time, Arc checked around the corner to make sure the coast was clear.

"Considering his lies regarding you, I wouldn't put any truth or trust in the rest of his words. We'll find out what really happened."

"If he shows up again. . . should we run, or no?"

"I'd prefer to run, to keep you safe in case of all the possible 'ifs.'"

"It's the poison," Pleia mused. They were passing through a garden now, run wild by weeds, yet still hauntingly quaint. Tools were scattered here and there as though the morning's work had been wrapt up in silence and disintegrated.

"Painful," Arc offered soberly. He turned his head to her. "I wouldn't want to face it without you, Pleia."

Pleia let out a shaky breath. As of yet, the green mist was nowhere else to be seen. That was something, at least.

"It causes the hallucinations," she speculated. "There's enough molecules spread thin to cause them. . . and the higher the concentration, the worse effects follow, it seems. Perhaps hallucinations played a role in what happened here."

"May well be. Pleia!"

He caught her as she tripped once again.

"Ah, it's the thorns," Pleia complained breathlessly, trying to kick the writhing branch away from her ankle. The leather of her boots kept them from putting her to sleep, this time.

Arc crushed it under his heel and swept her up and around his side as the patch of wriggling weeds became evident in the pavement's cracks.

"Ah, yes, you're a trip hazard again. Let's not have a repeat of Sleeping Beauty, shall we? Whatever would you do without me?"

He was smiling.

She laughed and did her best to keep an eye on the ground.

"That's a question we should put to Eridan, when we see him."

"Indeed, we should."

"Here's something that may help-"

Arc paused at a sign which seemed to have been a directional for tourists. Due to language barriers, symbols were used for locations instead; one seemed to be a church, another a star over waves: a symbol for the Starpool, they guessed. The arrow was pointing up the northernmost street, which seemed correct.

"Ahem, I'm still here," a cough sounded behind them.

Arc didn't stop to look, pulling Pleia up the hill at breakneck speed, lest she decide to pounce on the apparition once more. Footsteps were certainly audible, and one couldn't hear a hallucination so well – or could they? Yet they seemed to lose him for a minute as they were confronted by a dark passageway framed by an arch of carved seawaves.

Arc leaned over and brushed some lichen from a half-obliterated sign.

"Arr. . . arrr what?" He squinted, but the carvings were too old to read much.

"Oh, oh, this word means pool, I think," Pleia pointed to one farther down. "It's the same as in one of the names for the Starpool given on the columns."

Pleia studied their surroundings, but all she could remember were the faces she had been fascinated by.

"I don't remember coming this way. . . I don't know what way we came," she confessed. "I never saw those columns, either."

"It may be a shortcut, then. We'll get there. We know it's upwards."

Pleia looked up at the sky. The day was waning quickly.

"We don't have much time. If we get stopped again, we might not make it, it's still so far."

"Then we'll take the shortcut, and if we're not there in ten minutes, we'll come back this way."

Arc stepped in and took in the damp air, solidly murky path, and walked out again.

"Nope, I think not. I'm not taking you in there."

"The street probably *is* the straightest way," Pleia began, but Arc wasn't listening. His head was turned over his shoulder. He seized her arm.

"We just ran out of options."

He pitched them both into the darkened passageway as the cloud of poison rolled in amidst Antaré's running footsteps; a scream echoed from somewhere at sea.

They were running too swiftly to hear it, and too blinded by the darkness to keep themselves from falling and enduring a wild free-slide down the slick, sloping passage.

Arc grunted a little when they tumbled down a short flight of stairs to a jarring halt, but he kept Pleia from having a rough fall. Pleia glanced back up the slope as Arc pulled them both to their feet. Nothing was following them. She turned her attention to their surroundings.

A watery cerulean luminance filled the room in which they stood. Intricately carved stone framework stretched to the ceiling, holding back a wall of glass, and behind that, the sea, in an underwater grotto. A vast walkway encircled the aquarium-like setting, curving out of sight. Dampness filled the air, and algae, the cracks and crevasses in the stones.

Both found themselves turning from the eerie, rippling patterns cast across the walls to gaze into the grotto.

"This must be the chamber they built for the pleisiasaur," Arc surmised. His eyes followed every shadow, but the grotto was empty.

"Under the sea. . .
Haunts the beast of Seven Suns
Arcanum of the fallen night
Seven shattered suns
Setting in the endless sea. . ."

He exhaled and turned away.

"Ancient song from my ancestors," he said in reply to Pleia's glance. "I'm beginning to have an idea of why."

There was a distant ominous creaking and groaning, as of rusting metal and settling stone. Then nothing.

Pleia dropped her gaze to the path ahead with sudden fear that someone was there. No one.

Arc took her hand, looking into the face washed out by the greenish lighting.

"There will be other exits."

His voice echoed, emphasizing the vastness of the chamber.

She pressed his fingers.

"Let us go, then," she whispered. "I fear the setting sun."

They rounded the grotto, which proved to be more extensive than it seemed. It took a full ten minutes to reach the opposite side. There had been a number of presumable exits, some blockaded by stone, others by thick curtains of sea-moss, and the pathways behind were too steep to climb.

"Arc – will we have time?"

Her eyes were filling once more with distress. Unconsciously, she was squeezing his wrist, pulse after pulse to match her heartbeat.

"There's always enough time, Princess."

"But if we take too long-"

"It's accounted for."

His voice was always level, always quiet. She had that to lean on.

Shifting sounds, sounds of hissing, leaking seawater, and the drip-drip from above lent a haunted feeling to their surroundings. Against their own assurances, both found their gazes turning frequently upon the chamber, waiting for something to appear there.

"Hmm, no pleisiasaurs," was Arc's comment. "Probably died out, Princess."

All that noise, and the ringing of their footsteps, and it still seemed too quiet. Assurance was one thing; still they remained feeling as though they were being watched. Yet, no faces lingered here, in the corner of Pleia's eyes. She didn't stir to take her hands from where Arc clasped them on his arm, and neither did he.

"Arc!" Pleia heard herself exclaim, tightening her hold.

Arc halted at once and looked to her.

"I'm right here," he soothed her. "Are you alright?"

She caught herself and shakily nodded her head. They moved on.

Pleia's steps moved swifter, until she was fairly pulling her companion along. She knew she was unnerved. So did he. Only one found it a fault.

"Wait!"

The curve had halted, just for a moment, broken by an alcove set into the glass; from a crack in which ran a steady stream of water, crossing the path and draining into an old, fluted channel along the wall. There was a pedestal in that alcove, and from it had fallen a book – the kind in which one took notes.

"A rinnan book. . . that's odd."

"A what?" Pleia asked blankly.

Arc lifted the book gingerly, for the spine was rotting away.

"A rinnan book. Do they not teach you vocabulary at the Temple? Don't tell me that's another antiquated word we've saved. According to Eridan, there's quite a few."

"I . . . won't tell you then? But what is it?"

"Random, and it looks like a log of some kind," he said, cracking it open. "Of all the places to be – Pleia, this looks like the account we've been missing."

"That's suspiciously convenient – it's neither a logical nor safe place, considering the dampness – unless Ireo placed it here to be sure we'd find it."

"Hm, my thoughts exactly. Either way, it shall save us time at this point."

Arc was flipping through the log, scanning for anything resembling the end of the sculptured account. The log was written in the ancient text, but it wasn't too dissimilar from that studied by those in the Temple and in the forest alike.

Arc frowned, drawing Pleia's attention to another page.

"So, he was lying. Your forebear and Dà-El were protectors, not instigators."

The trouble had begun when Dà-El departed to check the kingdom's outposts, as he was prepared to make his promise to wed Gienna. His cousin, Lesaith – surely Antaré's ancestor, Arc noted - who was on visit in Alultaurari, tried to convince Gienna to wed him instead.

When she refused, he used her to threaten Tauré to step down as steward and began turning the people against their shepherdess. He began destroying all that was good in the kingdom while his men kept Dà-El from returning, laying siege to his outposts.

Lesaith robbed the poor, leaving them nothing to survive; homes were acquisitioned; all the profits of the harvest were taken for himself. The poor who came for the shepherdess' mercy were turned away before she could care for them, and the only men in the kingdom who received anything were those who gave bribes.

It was then that Tiran appeared, and warned Lesaith that should the tyrant-minded not change their ways and follow the commandments, enthroning both mercy and justice at their judgment-seat, there would follow disaster; but if they did so, there was hope that Deo would have mercy on some remnant of the tyrant's line.

Warnings were given by the other angels and by Maia:

Ireo: *Therefore thus saith the Lord: In every street there shall be wailing: and in all places that are without, they shall say: Alas, alas! and they shall call the wanderers to mourning. And in all the orchards there shall be wailing: because I will pass through in the midst of the city, saith the Lord.*

Ascheré: *Woe to them that desire the day of the Lord and His judgement: to what end is it for you? For you, that day brings darkness, not the light you craved for; no radiance haunts about it, only gloom.*

Maia: *Take the faithful and depart this city, for when the poison comes, not one will be left of those who have given in; they shall leave nothing among themselves, and turn upon each other as wolves, no matter the grace given them. Take the people, Dà-El, and build the city of Scier in a land far from here. Heal your people, and keep them strong; for if the weakness falls again, the poison which shall be withheld within this city shall be spread; and in that day, the only remedy will be to return here and find the grace lost.*

The age-old poison began to filter up from the cracks in the hill, turning the people against each other, changing the animals into beasts. By the time Dà-El returned, the sea was threatening to take the city over. The Tureis were doing their best to retain the warring, while Gienna was trapped in the city, doing her best with her star's gift, but was mortally wounded by Lesaith.

The pleisiasaur fell with the city, turning back into beast when the poison escaped; she was indeed the first to go, and her terrors made the situation far worse. It was too late to do anything but to leave with the prophecy and let the ocean and mist close in, sealing Alultaurari. The population had been a hundred thousand. Only ten thousand survived.

Arc slammed the book shut. The cloud of parchment particles swirled about them, but he was glaring at the wall. He was thinking of lies, and of ancestry, and of old legends that had been passed down through the Guardians, which began to find solid ground.

From them he knew the final piece of the tale, that Dà-El had saved Gienna and they had wed, founding the new city of Tygeta in the outer regions of the kingdom, after the sea had taken away much of the land to keep souls away from the island.

Many tales spoke of trapped souls - surely those who had fallen prey to the poison – who, only by weakness and not by grave fault, remained in a purgatorial state within the city's bounds.

Pleia, too, was lost in thought, but all the while, she had been glancing uneasily up and down the corridor. A sharp jab of the nerves in her scar turned her towards the glass.

XII

Ferocity

It took her a full ten seconds to realize that the grinning visage into which she was gazing was that of the pleisiasaur. Eyes that were orbs of sickly chartreusian light, a frilled crown of blood-red, and the seven star-scars like exploded craters etched in blood and lava, and a hundred woven teeth sharper than the shock of finding out the ocean had a breathable floor, and the sky was possibly blue.

"Aaaarc-"

He glanced up at her painfully stretched voice. With a gasp, he yanked her back from the glass.

"Is that thing *smiling*?"

"Yes, that's bad -"

"I know why – run!" He jerked her down the corridor as a cloud of green mist flooded the alcove. With the sound of renting rocks and ripping fibers, blackened vines drove towards them from wall and ceiling -

The pleisiasaur shot through the water, dark shadow zipping almost too swiftly to see, always ahead, far more massive than Pleia's living nightmares, and poison was at their heels -

The thorns tried in vain to catch her, but Arc repeatedly snatched her away.

"Pleia! Pleia!"

But it wasn't Antaré's voice echoing in her mind as the star burned with those on the pleisiasaur's brow.

Follow my voice, little one. Up the stairs!

"This way!"

Pleia pulled Arc back as a sheet of moss parted, revealing a narrow stairwell, into which they ducked. The curtain swung back behind them, sealing the entrance once more. The cacophony faded.

The two caught their breath. The only sound now was a familiar one. The stairway stretched out of sight.

"What do you know, a *shortcut*. It looks like the path to the Starpool," Arc murmured.

The ceiling of the secret passage was marked with many stars and waves, with repeating archways marked with stones, not unlike the warming stones, save in their glassy seafoam and aqua hues.

He took Pleia's arm, and they began to mount the stairs. Beyond the third doorway, it began to curve and spiral upwards, carving through the grotto.

It was a strange thing to look out the crystal-clad windows and see the ocean all about them. Every moment they tensed, awaiting glimpses of the pleisiasaur's face, but every window remained empty.

"It's strange... I felt something when I looked into its eyes," Pleia said softly, among their echoing steps. "A connection, as though I'd met it before."

"I expect Maia placed the Pleiades on her brow as she placed the star on yours. Even sinless nature will rise and fall because of Scier."

"I fear she has more to do than we think."

"If anyone can find the key to free her, it's you."

She met his eyes and felt the tumbling fears subside. The Starpool's song was growing ever nearer. Once she saw the Pleiades – the key to her hope, the hope of Celae, would be turned.

"Do you – still think the others are safe?" Pleia asked after a minute of silence.

Arc paused.

"I don't know. But I am glad Eridan found the ability to join us." He almost smiled. "Otherwise, I'd be concerned. He'll do whatever he has to for us to make it through this, as will I."

Eridan, in fact, was not alright, nor was Trissa. Dia, for her part, had vanished into the fog sometime after Arc's departure, yet, surely, she couldn't have been anxious for Pleia, not when the Princess had the Guardian's company.

It was Trissa who noticed the handmaid's absence, after what she later said was exactly three minutes of sleep. She snapped upright, noting that she and Eridan were the only ones left.

"Eri! Where is everyone?" she asked sharply.

Across the meadow, Eridan, too, sat up, having only closed his eyes for a minute.

"Oh, Dia!" he growled. "Arc went after Pleia. Dia has a bad habit of following, and none too closely."

He helped Trissa to her feet.

"We'd best go after her. I don't believe we're meant to stay here, anyhow."

"I second that motion," Triss muttered, shouldering her bow and catching up her cloak.

"It's only been ten minutes or so. At least they can't be too far apart."

"Mm," Trissa replied, eyes on the ground as she searched for indication of direction by bent grass blades. She stiffened.

"Eridan."

He crouched with her. The grass had been crushed, not merely bent, and dew pooled within the divets pressed into the soil.

"Something else is out here." She glanced uneasily in the direction the tracks led. "It's following Dia."

Of one mind, they ran. The fog was closing in and every step was half-questioned, but unforgiven. Until Eridan grabbed Trissa and held her back, stumbling.

"It's not after Dia," he rasped, and they dove in opposite directions as a massive bear crashed through the clouds, sucking the mist away before it swirled in again.

It was a twin to those from the forest, save that its body was a tangle of wood and vines, eyes like burning embers.

Trissa let loose an arrow into its right eye as it bellowed at Eridan's blade. The arrow only burnt, slowly, into ashes as it lodged there.

Eridan hacked away at one paw as it batted towards him, narrowly missing a flight halfway across the glade.

"Where are its roots?" Trissa cried, striving in vain to find something to aim at.

"Don't see any – just run, Tri! Find Dia, you can't help me!"

He ducked and drove his blade into the mass of the bear's stomach, where it jammed.

"Tri, just go!" he shouted when he saw her standing still. She grit her teeth and plunged into the fog, leaving the hunter to his prey.

The wood was tough and forgave every mark he made. What was driving it – certainly no shred of sense – some primordial spawn of poison, as had been the beasts of long ago? At least this one hadn't made it past the ancient incoming of the waves!

Jamming his sword once more into the briar-bear's side, Eridan used the creature's wrestling bulk to catapult himself onto its back. If tearing at its neck would influence its course, perhaps he could drive it into the sea - If he did not hear Trissa scream.

XIII

Identity

Some several hundred crumbling steps later, Arc and Pleia came to an amber-embedded door marked with silver swans and a great star like the one on Pleia's brow. A symbol of a rising sun over the sea was impressed upon it as if on wax; it had been braced by two marble columns, but one had fallen before it and blocked the path.

"This column will be a hard task in itself," Arc commented. He waved Pleia against the wall so she wouldn't be crushed, should he manage to shift it. He put his back to it and strained.

Pleia watched a moment and seeing that he was more likely to hurt himself before he moved the column far enough, she put her own little strength into it, and aided him to shove it a few feet farther from the door. An inch more, and it slid and rolled down the steps with a crash.

"There!" Arc sighed, glancing after it. "Come, let us see what's beyond this door." He pulled on the door, wrestling with the rusted bolt.

When it swung open at last, they beheld a gardened cloister with echoing walls, seemingly endless rows of columns, and streams of still-bubbling fountains.

"I know the way from here!" Pleia breathed feverishly, and her steps quickened almost to a run. The corridor opened onto the ancient spacious courtyard. Just as she had remembered, poison was absent; spring-fed streams sang with songbirds, and vines were hung with unnamed flowers and frosted berries.

Through the delicately-laced archways shone the cerulean sea, and before those walls lay the ovaline pool, with its lush frame of moss, phyla, and smooth sea glass embraced by twining vines. The water was the dark stillness of a sapphire, free of the clouds overhead.

The singing hum was all around them now, blending with the birdsong, and everything else seemed so far away. It was as though Antaré, the pleisiasaur, the poison, the thorns, were all in another world.

For a moment both stood, entranced, looking at the spot where the pool was set.

"Maia, Maia!" Pleia heard herself breathing, and her heart cried when no one stepped from among the flowers.

But the Starpool was there. It seemed as though it had been ages since she had last set eyes upon her stars, glowing in that pool. It had been like the promise of lush fruit at the end of summer, something that wasn't even a dream anymore, in Celae. The dehydration from a dream was real, but so, surely, was the promise.

Except – Antaré's fearful lies curled about Pleia's mind and made her afraid to look into the water.

Arc saw her fear and didn't feel the same. He drew her to the edge.

Nothing.

The indigo mirror remained reflectionless of the stars hidden above.

Pleia hesitantly tapped the water's surface, but the only ripples were the ones she cast.

"There are no stars," she faltered. She raised her eyes to the sky, but it was filled with clouds of darkening gray. The sun was sliding ever farther into their depths.

Arcturus crouched at the pool's edge and looked across at her.

"I don't see any stars. But I do see Pleia."

She met his gaze, but her mind was numbing in confusion.

"The Pleiades were my hope...now I can't see them. There's nothing here! If I can't follow them, how will we help anyone? They were the only key she gave me, Arc!"

She was almost in tears.

"One doesn't need hope once what's looked for is found...Pleia...*des.*"

Pleia stared at him. "Arc-"

"'*These stars are yours, as they are mine. . . for this treasure, you will suffer great sorrow, as I have.*' You've been the kingdom's star ever since you arrived at the Temple, even to those of us banned from the kingdom. It's you who has been drawing us out of danger, given your life for the kingdom's healing. You saved me from the poison. You *are* our hope, Pleia."

He rose and stretched his hand out to her across the water.

"You've doubted yourself for too long. I think Scier says it's time for you to know who you are: *His* Pleiades."

He looked into her widened eyes, finding them as deep as the pool at their feet, yet shimmering with the very stars that hadn't fallen there.

"Trust me. . . trust yourself, Pleia," he whispered, and in a daze, Pleia reached her hand across the pool and laid it in his.

The water rippled. This time it was not from a touch, nor even a breath. Something was glowing there – and it wasn't the Pleiades.

A woman's face smiled as a triangle of stars crowned her hair – Ireo, Tiran, and Ascheré.

As a star must burn before it grants light, so must the soul be broken, little one, before the star within you may heal.

The water rippled; Maia faded, leaving the crown upon the hair of Pleia's reflection.

"But . . . I haven't been broken, Arc," she breathed.

"I'm here. Whatever happens, Pleia, no one will truly leave your side."

She looked at their hands, still clasped, and stooping, touched her lips to his fingers.

"I know."

Ascheré sparkled in the water as with a whisper.

"You know . . . more than you think."

"Eriiiii?!"

Trissa's repeated scream rent the fog as with a veil, or was it the second bear that had pounded out of nowhere?

"Tri!"

Eridan yanked violently on the vines he had half torn from the briar-bear's neck. It bellowed and swung its head, stumbling in the direction he had pulled, but there was no time, not when Trissa was in need.

Ascheré, Tiran, Ireo – consider these bears yours now! he thought.

He jerked his mount aside, sending it crashing head-on into the newcomer, and vaulted in the moment of collision, leaving himself to scramble up from the dewy grass and charge in the direction of the call.

"Tri!"

"Eriii, help me!"

Her voice was creeping higher with each cry that bounced off the trees.

Where was she?!

Every cry was drawing the bears in his direction. At least the echo was throwing them off, ever so slightly.

"Tri, I can't find you!"

He slapped aside the clinging vines swinging from the trees. He had an inkling, just for a moment, that they were trying to stop him, but that was the mere imagination of fear.

He turned his head and heard sobbing now, seemingly on his right. He struck out through the foliage. The bears could be heard crashing through the trees, somewhere in the east. Catching branches, vines and ferns felt endless as he fought through them, trying to pinpoint Trissa's location. A hidden tree root nearly pitched him headfirst into the clearing.

"Tri!"

She had fallen, sprawling against a moss-tainted log, two snaking vines coiled around her, preventing her from rising.

He hacked them in twain, and they fell back.

"Tri, Tri, are you hurt?"

He lifted her up. Her face was streaked with tears, and she was shivering fit to fall apart. Her white lips trembled so much she could scarcely get any words out.

"He – he – he tried to kill us – not again -"

"You mean – the man who had hurt you?"

He held her face in his hands. The scalded look in her eyes was answer enough.

Yet it couldn't be – Arc had told him, privately, that the man had later fallen in a skirmish at the forest's edge.

Triss knew that, too.

"I – I saw Ayeleth, playing – he tried to kill her – I can't have seen them, Eri, I can't -"

She broke off in a sob, in part because her logic couldn't end the trauma.

Eridan smoothed her cheeks, wiping away the tearstains. He was hyper-aware of the pawthumps that were closing in.

"I'll keep you safe now. Nothing can get past me this time, and I'll never let any man hurt you."

She managed to stop crying.

"I thought the island would be safe."

"We all hoped so, Tri, for a little while."

"The bears," Trissa muttered, straining to gather herself together as she reached for her stave.

"We can't run from them. Trust the angels and I to deal with them."

So saying, he arose, for he could hear their breathing from the edge of the clearing.

"Quick, in here," he said, and swung the girl into a deep hollow below tree roots, before she could object.

Drawing his blade, he backed into the center of the glade. He didn't have long to wait. In only a heartbeat the briar-bears crashed their full fury on him, the only grace being their smaller size and the vines he'd already cut. Yet even a champion could only last so long before he was side-swiped, clawed and crushed against the tearing bark of a tree.

Trissa watched in horror, feeling as though the roots arching above her were her own, locking her into the ground.

She tried to draw back her bowstring or to clasp her stave, but her fingers had no strength.

"Come on, come on!" she exhaled shakily.

But with every blow Eridan received, she lost strength rather than gaining it.

"No, no, why?" Trissa wept, clenching her fingers, trying to force some stability into her muscles. Promises or no promises, he couldn't make it alone.

"Tiran, Ascheré, Ireo, please! He's the only one I'm not afraid of – don't. . . don't. . ."

Her fingers willed to grip her stave and she lashed out like lightning, enough to make the larger bear turn its wooden head and leave the champion to fall to the ground.

There was no forgiving. Not before, not now. She would burn them into ashes if it were the last thing she did.

XIV
Penalty

"Ascheré?"

The angel smiled. He moved around the pool from its head, as the two remaining stars in the reflection's crown winked and faded away.

He was clad in eburnean threaded with iridescence and gold; his gilded breastplate was graced by his sparkling star, beating as an irised heart.

"I am. We've been awaiting you for a long time, little star."

"You can't be Sirius!" Arcturus exclaimed.

Ascheré raised an eyebrow and laughed.

"If I weren't, would I be as fond of your humor?"

Arc grinned and desisted.

"Vërtë," he murmured, relinquishing his grasp on Pleia's hand.

Ascheré turned his eyes of morning-sky down upon Pleia, whom he fairly dwarfed.

"Are you real? Antaré isn't, yet he is," she began fearfully, and dropped her eyes from his face to his star.

His gaze was loving as he as he answered, "Yes, Antaré is poison, but far more than the word; I am real, little star, far more than my name."

"But how am I to know, when I couldn't tell with him? What if this is all. . . just a dream, or poison?"

"Perhaps you don't, Pleia. . . .Perhaps that is your test."

As Ireo had been to her, so she could hope he would be.

She smiled slowly for him. His eyes sparkled and he drew her close until her head rested on the star. Folding his arms around her, he returned his attention to Arc.

"Arcturus. You must go, and leave the city, for your sister has need of you. Leave Pleia under my wing, Guardian, and do not fear for her. If you do not, you will not be able to save your sister from taking revenge - and her life."

He raised one hand to the southwestern wall and the ivy swung aside, and a patch of the wall vanished amidst a glaucous haze.

"You will find the path swifter now."

Arc paled, but didn't move, calculating the chances of Ascheré being as Pleia had feared, but the maiden no longer felt that fear.

"Go," Ascheré said gently, but firmly. "Trust her to me. I will guard her until your return."

Arc believed. He set his jaw and took his leave at a run, leaving Pleia safe, alone, with Ascheré.

The earth was growling beneath the lumbering paws of the briar-titans. Trissa's violence had been unleashed as it would have been in Archidron without Eridan's arrival. The revived anger of her pain kept the attackers away from him.

Their own fire might not burn them - but hers would. One of the hand-held warming stones was in the pack at her waist; now it was in her hand, and she was striking it against the rock wall, hard enough to produce a flame.

Dianthe had been wiser than she knew to braid the grass those many long nights ago. They had dried now and were only too flammable. Fireballs were exactly what she needed.

She balled up and lit those twists which remained, stave spinning in one hand all the while, threatening to mar the bears' vision if they came too close.

All those days in Tania, few had been able to excel her marksmanship, and that was a consolation to her now, as she repeatedly made her mark and was rewarded by bursts of flame. The briar-bears snarled and tried to put out their fiery coats, to no avail; branch and briar began to burn away, peeling back in ashes -

She had damaged them enough to make out their amber hearts, nestled in a thorny frame.

"May you die for all the evil that you are!" Trissa whispered, and leapt from the ledge, placing herself within reach of tooth and claw. One blow of her stave to each was all she would need. Then, maybe, a little easing of the pain. . . a little safety for her to take care of Eridan.

There were wounds she'd nursed for too long, that might just heal a little – or tear open, and maybe that would be satisfying, if those claws caught her, too.

Her anger was interrupted.

A spear hurtled into the earth between the guardian and her foes.

"Tri! Spare yourself of revenge."

A rattling growl through clenched teeth confirmed her brother's arrival. Mere man though he was, whatever dire threat he uttered edged the bears back and away from his sister. A hiss sent them begrudgingly out of the clearing.

Trissa dropped her stave and sank to the ground, trying to let go, every cell beginning to shake. It was as though it were her blood that had spilled from Eridan, as it had been hers that spilled from Ayeleth.

Arc leapt down and lifted her with a quick glance into her eyes that told him enough; he fairly carried her up the slope to where Eridan lay and dropped beside him.

"Eri. . . Eri! You're not supposed to be able to get hurt," Triss whispered, taking his head into her lap.

He almost laughed, coughing.

"I never said that."

"Well, you can't die, because I will – I'll go fight those bears to death again myself if you do!"

"Triss," Arc sighed.

Eridan choked.

"Well then, I'm hardly able to die, am I," he said with a laughing grimace. Blood was running out of his mouth.

Arc was frowning as he did his best to staunch the blood from the stomach wounds.

"Verily, you'd better not be planning on going anywhere, because the angels will have something to say about that."

Eridan woke up enough to scowl.

"Tell me you didn't leave Pleia."

"I left her with Ascheré."

"Dia?"

"Haven't seen her."

"Lovely, no, I'm not going anywhere -" he tried to sit up but fell back, vomiting blood.

"No, don't try," Trissa breathed, pressing her forehead against his, no longer asking why she couldn't stop shaking.

A breath blew through the glade and rustled the leaves.

"Arcturus. Stand away from him."

The voice was gentle in command, the soft ripple belonging to the name before they saw the face.

Arc stepped away.

Tiran knelt in the moss and brought the light of his right hand over Eridan's heart.

"Now is not the time to fight, Champion of Scier," he murmured. "Let go, for peace is the only way to heal."

Yet his eyes were on Trissa's.

The tenseness fell away, and Eridan stopped struggling to breathe steadily.

The angel lifted his left hand and touched his index and middle fingers to Trissa's brow.

"You are the same," he said with a tender smile, and Trissa let her shoulders fall as his energy flowed between them, the anger fading, like an ocean of clear, golden air.

Eridan sat up and looked into Tiran's face. His thanks were silent because they would not be voiced. But his concern broke out, barely above his breath.

"Will she be alright?"

The angel smiled, almost amused. He turned his eyes to Trissa.

"Whichever one you mean. . . I'll take it as all three. . . they'll be alright. Now."

He swept to his full height and looked down at them.

"Now," he repeated. "You must enter the city in all haste, lest your own fall. I will be there, as will my brothers be."

He stepped back. Golden faded into green and he was gone.

Arc lifted the couple to their feet.

"Alright, you almost-one. Let's run."

XV

Toxicity

Pleia met Ascheré's eyes as the wall sealed shut behind Arcturus. In the pool at their feet, she could see that the sun was sinking below the city's parapet and that time was running out.

"Now?"

She wasn't sure what she was asking.

He was silent, looking across the sea.

"Now," he replied at last.

Pleia fought panic as she related her fears and confusion to him.

"The others – must they be hurt for me? Will they be safe?"

"That is not for me to tell you, little star."

Pleia glanced out towards the meadow. She could not see where the others had gone and could only guess at what was taking place.

"You said I know more than I think," she sighed, "and yet I don't understand. I don't understand anything, and I'm afraid -"

She hesitated.

"I know it's not of fault, and I'm sure you know already, but I fear that all this is mere imagination, or hallucination – that my dreams were only that, that I'm not really here, and they – are only a dream," she finished with trembling lips.

Ascheré laid his hand on her hair.

"Sometimes, seeing is not believing; sometimes, it is belief that grants sight. Sometimes, the only grace is hope, and all one can do is hope blindly and will to serve Scier when nothing seems right. If your hope is good, then it is good, and Scier's hand will shelter you if your hope is not in truth. If you should forget, Maia is man's mother in faith, little one, in her faith and hope of what seems impossible."

"But does it apply to my love for them? Or is it that much less important? I don't know, I just don't know! I feel a failure for not knowing."

Ascheré turned from gazing into the pool.

"Was it ever a crime not to know? Or only something to endure?"

Pleia lowered her gaze in understanding as he had raised his. This, too, calmed the churning sea. Yet, it felt all too slow. She clenched her hand and tried to find what it was that she was missing.

"Fear is your enemy, Pleia. Do not fall to its urge to run against time, for that shall only speed the clock. There are many who pray that you'll be strong now, strong for them and for Scier."

"I don't want to be strong," she whispered back. "I want to lean on somebody's shoulder and have them hold my head when I can't."

If you lost your anxiety, little one, you would see what you have gained. Find yourself in my heart, and within my heart you shall find my Son.

Pleia raised her head in surprise, and Ascheré was smiling.

"Maia? Please, tell me! I'm not the girl who stood here, all those years ago. I've seen too much...! We all have," she sighed wearily. "It should have been the way it was...but men are foolish and hateful, against their nature, and look where we place ourselves then!"

The only reply was a rippling sigh, which might have been wind across the water.

"Maia," Pleia whispered again, but there was nothing else, and Ascheré gave no motion, either.

The sense of something evil was still stirring in her mind, and she seemed to feel shadows that flitted through the deep at the city's feet. The moon remained out of sight, cast from favor by the earth's shadow, and wherever she looked, the entrapping mist began to thin. The poison was gathering, concentrating in the city streets, growing equally invisible to the eye as the mist wall. Everything was escalating, and her heartbeat with it.

Ascheré stirred.

"Pleia. Arc is on his return; I must leave you now, and return to our Lady. You will be safe until his arrival, in a moment's time."

He dropped his hand on her hair again.

"Remember what I have said, sweet star. I will see you again."

He breathed softly on her forehead and was gone.

"Pleia?"

Arc's voice rang out with a note of urgency. He spun around the corner of the colonnade and halted, wild-eyed. He ran to her and gripped her shoulders with a look that frightened her.

"Why are you alone? Where's Ascheré? Have you found it?"

Pleia's troubled eyes stared into his as she slowly shook her head.

"He only just left, for you were returning. Where are the others?"

Arc exhaled shakily, glancing over his shoulder, and throwing a look to every corner of the courtyard.

"The poison took them as we entered the city. Listen to me! I have to keep you safe until the time comes. I'll get you to higher ground, we'll have a little time; it's coming up from below."

"Dia?"

It was his turn to shake his head.

"No one's seen her."

"Dia. . . she can't-"

Arc shook her gently.

"The angels are looking after her. Now, come!"

Catching her hand, he ran her out of the courtyard and up a winding stepstone path towards the city's steeple – the joint palace and cathedral, every turret marked by Scier's stars, the doorways guarded by the angel-trio, and every bolt locked by the Pleiades.

Arc stumbled and caught Pleia to his side.

A xanadu-hued veil fogged the opposite archway, curling into the plaza to intercept the grand staircase. Whispering, twisted laughter sounded horribly like the voices of their fallen companions.

"Pleia, go!" Arc urged. "It's hunting you! I'll keep it away."

"Arc-"

"Pleia! When it attacks, the whole of the cloud halts, that's how I was able to escape. You'll be able to get away. Go!"

"Arc, no! You can't – carry everything," Pleia whispered brokenly. "I can't – lose you too, don't break me, please."

Arc stooped so their eyes were level.

"Pleia. . . I carry what I can. I'm afraid you are carrying more than you know."

He smiled softly and touched her cheek.

"I trust you to save us. You'll save us, Princess. Now go, and stay safe until Maia heals you!"

He gave her a push, and as she ran for the stairs and he for the fog, she looked back.

Arcturus was swallowed by the cloud. It churned to a halt.

Pleia closed her eyes in pain.

The great doors swung open behind her. She ducked inside, and an unseen hand locked the massive bolts in place.

She was alone.

Alone.

XVI
Radiancy

The halls were dark. The weighted, once-rich, brackened velvet draperies rustled as they hung from soaring ceilings to marbled floor. Watery shimmers rippled across the surfaces, some luminant liquid channeled decoratively in patterns along floor and wall.

The graven sun on the gilt door ribbed into Pleia's back as she sat, curled up in the darkness.

The palace was warm from the day's sunrays, but her skin crawled as with pouring raindrops. That's what her breath sounded like, raggedly, in her own ears.

She tried to work through her pain, but she was lost. Voices swirled around her, her companions', and yet not. They had been bent out of focus and marred, almost to the point of being someone else.

She couldn't bear to think of them, so good, being twisted and under the power of poison. It couldn't be, what grave weakness did they have? Or was it none, as with the many who had fallen in Alultaurari?

For a moment she felt as in a fever, that she wasn't where she thought, that she was delusional in the Temple and the door pressing into her was that of her own bedroom. Yet, was that any better? To believe that Arcturus and Trissa were only phantoms of a daydream?

Her breath trembled and shuddered on the air; an echo swirled around the closing of the door. Pleia stirred and pulled herself away. No, the poison was there, and she was here.

Broken, yet she had to try rather than cry. How far did the poison seep into the soul? How far would Arc's sacrifice go?

"Oh, Maia!" Pleia gasped, and her song tumbled from her lips in the only plea she could make.

> *Mother, I have wandered ever far*
> *Your stars are fading out of reach*
> *This sea is too vast, hear my plea!*
> *I know I've strayed from your star*
> *I've fallen too far!*

Something echoed through the halls, faintly, reverberating from the distant ceilings, wafted as on a breeze.

A voice, was it? A song of no words, haunting, yet as though she'd known it before, but it wasn't the echo of her own.

Her breath trembled in and out through her lips and she set them, turning towards the fading melody. Whether it might be a phantom did not matter, when she had nowhere else to go, no trail to follow. Somewhere, deep within the walls of the palace lay the only answer she was given.

She drew herself to her feet and drifted up a staggered set of stairs into the grand hall, where vibrant reds and blues chased through the shadows in only a memory of its once-glory. The luminant braceways were the only light she had; she moved slowly, hesitating at every step, lest a stone be loose, or debris litter the ground before her feet.

She walked through in silence. All was eerily quiet; still, the quiet of a safe place. The palace seemed unravaged by the tragedy, save for the ruin of abandon. Perhaps the intertwining of church and palace could be the answer.

The call had ended.

She stopped, one glint of light glancing off a darkened frame, binding a portrait of a king and queen.

It was Dà-El and his Gienna, engagement ring sparkling, for it was a real diamond set within the canvas.

They were crowned by diadems of sunset and ocean – his of fiery sunstone and garnet, hers of rosy jasper, moonstone, verdant agate, and pearl. They were blinding, yet softened by ages of dust and sea-air. And yet it wasn't so much the crowns but the star upon Gienna's brow, framed by her diadem, that held Pleia's gaze.

If Gienna had failed – was it failure? Would she, Pleia, find failure, too? But was answering a call ever deemed failure, no matter which way it went. . .?

"Pray for me," she whispered, and hardly had it broken the stillness when a whisper answered down the hall. She turned.

Somewhere in the gloom-like shadows, two figures turned back, poised before what she'd thought had been a dead end.

For only a breath, the light passed over their faces, transparently transposed from the portrait's like-nesses. But it was only a moment, and Dà-El and Gienna turned and vanished.

Now Pleia was not sure that it was a wall that stood there. She felt her way through the dark, finding broken statues lying scattered, until she stood before that same dead end. It was covered by a heavy hanging, scarcely visible; she put out her hand and it moved back at her touch.

Not a wall, but a passage; and stepping through, ahead was a door, or remnant of one; columns had toppled as in the stairwell, and the tapestry which had hidden it fell in tatters over the wreckage.

Pleia carefully lifted this aside, rust falling from the lintel overhead, and squeezed through the narrow place. A sound of murmuring sing-song came from beyond.

The room which met her eyes contrasted the first with as much ethereal light as the former had darkness; the vaulted ceiling held by branching trees of verdant jasper, amongst walls of hushed sea green reflected in the pearled agate underfoot.

Before a pooling drapery of byssus was the face she'd been praying to see, and in the Lady's arms nestled the Bright Star, Scier, with His heart of sunlight filling the room brighter than Ascheré's star; and around the throne were those three stars which had crowned her hair.

Pleia halted a moment, afraid it was, as had been all other things she thought, only a vision, a shape that with the setting sun would flee. She had no capacity for that fear; it was pushing at her mind, making her feel as though it were weighted and empty. She gave up trying to worry, trying to cry, trying to find answers, and let go into a hand that could carry it all.

Her gaze entreated the vision to be true.

The woman arose from the throne where she'd been gracefully settled, shifting the Little Light in her arms.

"My little one. . . ! come to me." Her voice was the breaking and the safe haven Pleia had longed for, and she went, weeping, into the Mother's arms as she sank down on the stairs. The girl felt the silken hand on her hair as her head dropped to Maia's knee.

The rush of time had stopped. The reddening rays of the sun seemed to still in their tread across the room. Even Maia's lullabies lingered on the air. All thoughts seemed quiet save the one for which she had come.

"I don't want to ask why," she whispered.

Maia stroked her hair.

"My sorrowful little one. . . all that you wish for is in His heart. . . is there any need to fear, then? Do you understand the simplicity that a human can do the inhuman at the call of the Divine? The silence you have heard all this time was I, at your side, for no call is needed save at a distance. All that was needed was in time; all that has happened has been for the moving of grace. You have been blinded, Pleia, for it is your love and your alignment with, and openness to the Little Light, which you have been unable to recognize through your fears. Let those fears fall, now. . . know that you are loved, and you've not been wrong in searching."

Pleia found her chin cupped gently in Maia's hands and lifted; she read the echo of tears in Maia's smiling eyes.

"You alone have been born for this, for such a time as this. Do not doubt what Scier has done, for you alone, with the stepping stones given by those you love, can save His people from this poison."

"Can I?"

"You are more capable than you know."

"How?"

"Now that you're found, there is no worry."

Maia pressed her lips to the star on Pleia's brow and as it shimmered, motioned the three guardians forward.

Ascheré stretched out his hand and touched the star.

"To you I give my grace of enlightenment of hearts. I will be your sword and shield before Scier."

Ireo came behind him, and stooping over the maiden, did likewise.

"I grant to you my grace of the gentling of beasts; whether he be man or animal, you will share my hands, my eyes, and my tongue."

Then came Tiran with a smile, and as the others had, he blessed her, saying, "Receive the fullness of your grace, Pleia, with my grace of the purging of poison, be it that of life or death. Your heart will be as mine and be under my guard."

Maia sealed those graces with a kiss, and the Little Light placed His hand over it. Pleia began to feel an energy coursing through her, ripping away all fear, doubt, and confusion, leaving clarity so deep and still that even a turning of phantoms wouldn't have fazed her. For once in her life, she was truly as she had been made.

Her brow felt that a heavy crown had lifted, and as she looked at her hands, a starlit glow crept up them and washed over her, turning seafoam to pearl.

As she raised her hands, a light reflected in the vambraces that was neither the setting sun nor that of Little Light's heart.

The star had awakened.

The Pleiades were free.

XVII
Polarity

The grand doors thundered open to let Pleia through. She stood and surveyed the city which was falling into darkness. There was only a shroud of light left within the outer court, and none was reflected by a poison cloud.

Pleia's brow creased. Where the cloud, and where its prisoners? Had it all faded into invisibility?

She descended the stairs and crossed the courtyard, stepping through the archway into which Arcturus had plunged. Nothing but an ivy-coated garden greeted her in the inimitable silence of loneliness. Or was it so?

The leaf-strewn pathway led through the hanging gardens, and eventually, down to the harbor. That was where she needed to go.

Pleia followed the moss-trod flagstones through the solar and lunar gardens and would have entered the lower celestial terraces if she had not sensed someone nearby.

Pleia turned back – no one was in sight, but she ducked through overhanging moonflower vines and found what once had been a restful tea patio, with tarnished table and chairs; and the sole occupant was Arcturus.

"Arc!"

Pleia lifted him gently from where he slumped upon the wrought-iron table.

"Arc. . . Arc, awaken."

He focused dazedly on her face, more precisely, on the glowing star.

"Pleia?"

His face was as haggard as if he'd been through a war, but his eyes lit softly. Pleia brushed the sweat-dampened hair from his forehead and laid her hand there. There was no poison in him.

"Oh, oh Arc! I had feared you were lost," she breathed.

"It held me captive, but it seemed unable to do much else," he managed. "Tried to. . . kill me, I think. . . tormented me in the least."

"Oh, Arc. . .Your sacrifice preserved you from the worst, and you have saved more than yourself." She kissed his forehead and placed her hand on his heart. "You were right to trust what I could not."

Tiran, let your grace be as mine; heal this heart most worthy.

She sang a soft ripple of notes; the ones she'd always known. The breeze echoed, ruffling Arc's hair. Pleia gently kissed his brow once more and blew away the pain.

Arc sighed and returned to himself at once.

"Is it gone? Is it done, Pleia?"

"No; before I may, I must be certain that all of you are safe," she answered gravely.

He got to his feet, having again calculated her thoughts.

"Well, then, you're right that it was heading to the harbor. It seems that's where Eridan and Trissa are."

"Then that is where this is meant to end," Pleia replied, raising her eyes to the painted sky.

"Thirty minutes," Arc said quietly.

"There is always enough time. It will be well," she murmured, half to herself.

Arc took her arm and together they made their way down the city slope.

The harbor was eerily placid. Waves rolled like caressing hands against the pier and the carcasses of rotting ships at shore. The ominous whispers of water and wind were as so many voices, marking danger lurking from behind, then from a half-crushed shipment of pearls, once well-valued, now spilling upon the ocean floor.

Arc's hand pressed against Pleia's back, shielding her from behind; his eyes restlessly roved, probing the quickly deepening shadows. The evening sun lit the harbor, blinding from the water, as it hung suspended atop the horizon.

If that silken thread of time were cut, it would plunge into the sea and take Celae and her enemies with it, submerged in a watery grave in which neither time nor dawn could make a difference.

The harbor was too still to be their known destination. The pair stopped at the crown of the pier. There was nothing to see, save the maddeningly dwindling light.

The star tingled faintly, effervescently, warning -

A sound of the drawing of a breath by steel and their eyes met those of Eridan. They were smoldering ice, and sick. His blade was raised to strike.

"Eridan, no!" Arc said sharply.

But the once-champion only curled his lip from behind his blade as he raised it before his face.

His smile was more akin to Ahknett's than the one Pleia and Dianthe had always loved.

"But where is Trissa?" Arc muttered, eyes fastened on Eridan's every minute movement, feeling for the moment of attack.

Faintly, shifting in the mirror of Eridan's sword, Pleia saw something.

The star burned and Pleia pitched herself and Arc aside as Trissa hurtled to the place they'd been, her stave likely to have cracked both their skulls.

Arc used his spear to block Trissa's attack, parrying Eridan in between blows, blocking their path to Pleia as he strove to defend her. Yet he was being pushed back towards the water.

"Ideas?"

"They remember themselves enough not to kill us, don't fight them fully!"

Arc reluctantly let his guard down a trifle; Trissa felled him and tried to pin him down as Eridan seized Pleia by her arms. As swiftly as he did so, he fell helpless to harm her. He became quiet and sullen, gripping her arms as he looked into her eyes.

"'Dan, 'Dan. . . ! You don't need to hurt me. Wake up, Eri-!"

Something ripped up the boardwalk beneath their feet, throwing them violently apart as the water surged between them.

Any effect she might have had on Eridan was erased. Arc managed to escape from his sister, and sweeping Pleia up from where she'd fallen, yanked her through a maze of somehow-existent crates.

"Arc, I need their eyes fixed on me!"

He pulled her to a sheltered spot and glanced out from behind a stack of barrels. Their pursuers had already plunged into the labyrinth to find them.

"Easy enough, if you subtract the 'they're *apparently* not trying to murder you, and that's why they're looking at you, and we have thir-no, twenty-five minutes,' part."

"Then let's keep them still. I'm certain they won't have the ability to harm us."

"Unless they get us from a distance," Arc muttered.

He took her hand and they retreated further into the maze. Arc quietly pried at some of the dilapidated boxes, hunting for anything of use, but the contents were equally decayed.

They could hear Eridan smashing his sword hilt into similar crates, ensuring none served to hide his quarry; as for Trissa, Arc knew all too well how silent she could be.

"Not safe here," he murmured in Pleia's ear, for his sister might already be poised to pounce.

But Pleia didn't need to be told. She already had a sinking feeling, as though what was behind them was no empty space for the ocean to flail against.

Arc felt it, too. They turned to look.

Silent as a revenant, acid-venom eyes were level with theirs as vapor curled from between its dripping teeth. The bloody frill flared open.

Without a breath to spare, Arc dove and rolled, taking Pleia with him as Ahknett's head destroyed every crate in the vicinity, sending splinters and sawdust flying.

Arc dragged Pleia down the boardwalk, but Eridan and Trissa were closing in, and Ahknett's neck meant they weren't safe anywhere they went – unless it were in the shallows.

A derelict barque had settled there, line still tied about the piling. Arc gave the rotten wood a kick, freeing the line, and catapulted them both onto the ship's deck – momentarily safe from their earthbound pursuers. As for Ahknett, it was shallow enough that she could scarcely do more than hiss within range of the ship's bow from the other side of the pier.

"We'll never have enough time at this rate," Arc stated, pulling Pleia to her feet after further testing the deck under his own weight.

"There will be."

Pleia was searching for any sign of the poison, but there was only the vapor of Ahknett's breath. Arc read Pleia's gaze.

"Is it in the pleisiasaur?"

"Not all of it," Pleia replied slowly. She could sense that much, but where the majority of it was, she could not say.

Arc bumped her arm.

"We're about to have company. Let's get below deck."

As he swung the cabin door shut, Trissa pole-vaulted onto the bow and cast a line to Eridan. Arc and Pleia might as well have been in a net now.

Inside the ship, it was murky, and the wood creaked menacingly at every step. Somewhere below, waves pulsed tinnily, trapped within the broken hull. Voices came now and again, ghosts whose seenless hands sent tattered curtains rippling.

There was a stairway leading down from the living quarters; they took it and found themselves in what had once been passenger's cabins, but the walls had fallen to dust, and it steeply sloped, falling into the flooded hold. The water was illuminated, not unlike Ahknett's grotto.

They slipped down against one remaining wall and tried to stay out of sight.

"Please, tell me those aren't sharks," Arc whispered.

Pleia looked to the swimming shadows.

"I fear I can't tell you," she answered, as the rafters squeaked under weight.

"All the things I never thought I'd have to handle – no matter for now. When those two come down, we'll try to immobilize them."

Thankfully, the floor they were on wasn't fully collapsed; barrels of what once had been provisions still lined the walls where the floor was intact. They were held in check from the slope by sturdy netting pinned to wall and floor. These days, it was easy to tear these out, but it came at a price. The barrels toppled into the water with a splash, voiding stealth. The footsteps overhead came on rapidly, fading towards the stairway.

"At least they're coming," Arc muttered, and they ducked under the stairwell, ready to snap the net taut and catch the pair on the way down.

Only, there was a musty crack of timber and the rafters over the pool gave way -

"'Dan!" Pleia exclaimed and dropped the net.

XVIII
Petrify

Eridan had caught onto one barely sturdy rafter; the sharks, as poisoned as Ahknett, grew agitated below him.

"Eri!" Trissa's white face appeared through the gap as she tried to pull him back, without falling through herself.

"Tri! Are you free?" Arc called up to her, inching around the pool's edge.

"I – I don't know," she moaned feverishly, pulling at Eridan's arm. "Don't let him fall!"

She might have been partially free in the least, but Eridan was still throwing poisoned glares at those below him.

"It's alright, Tri, Pleia will be able to free you." Arc turned to Pleia. "Help me net some of these barrels!"

But Pleia knelt and laid her hand on the water's surface. The star at once shone and sparkled across the water's surface; the agitation of the beasts began to cease, until the water was calm.

Arc cast the net out and managed to drag a few of the floating barrels together, making something of a platform.

It was hardly in place before there was another crack of failing timber and Eridan fell, Trissa tumbling after with a shriek. She missed the barrels and surfaced growling, fighting the weight of her quiver; but her eyes were locked on Pleia's.

Pleia held out her hand.

"Come, Trissa. Give me your hand. It's *alright*, Tri." Her voice was soft in command as she repeated the girl's name, more firmly each time.

Trissa paused, cocking her head, and nearly went under. One of the sharks swam past and bumped into her with its fin. She snapped.

"Sharks, sharks, *sharks!* Where's Dianthe to teach that they aren't bananas?" she yelped, and Pleia pulled her in.

There was a splash as Eridan snapped with her and lost his balance, and nearly his sword.

"What in the heavens, would someone please tell me how we got here now? Are we drowning?" he spluttered. "Wait, Dianthe *still* isn't here?"

"Thank you, one-half, for saving us time," Arc drawled, hauling him in. "Long story short, we have twenty minutes, an angry sea monster, and no knowledge of where the poison is. We also have the Pleiades."

He smiled at Pleia as Eridan shook the water from his hair, also shaking his confusion.

"At any rate, welcome aboard, let's get out before we drown."

Which was going to be easier said than done, now that Ahknett's head rammed into the prow below the waterline, shoving the wreck back into the merchant vessel at its stern, and equally ripping the aft open. She had wriggled her head below the pier, giving her access to the sunken levels.

Barrels crashed down in a cascade of sea. The only way out was into the neighboring ship's bow.

"Go, go!"

Arc shoved Pleia, Eridan dragged Trissa, and they found themselves dodging chests, crates, and anemones as they bounced from one bobbing barrel to another, as Ahknett destroyed the second vessel, then the third. Trissa tore a byssus curtain from one of the captain's cabins as they ran, slinging it over her shoulder.

Thankfully, here the prow pointed to the sky over the shallows. The group managed to escape out onto the pier before realizing they had reached the opposite, deeper end of the harbor where the loading dock lay; and there Ahknett could reign. That she did and separated the couples before they'd so much as drawn a collective breath. The only escape was if they climbed the staggering stone walls towards the city line.

They didn't see Trissa fall back, the curtain over her shoulders. The silver glimmer was akin to that of Pleia's garments, and so the creature lost sight of her primary prey. Trissa became separated from the group instead, luring Ahknett towards the end of the dock, away from the others.

Feeling Trissa take her hand from his, Eridan glanced back from climbing the wall.

"Triss! Ack, she's worse than Dianthe," he growled, as Arc and Pleia realized what was happening.

Eridan was the first to reach her, weaving between the stone columns of the quay to avoid Ahknett's teeth and the waves she sent crashing over the pier. Trissa yelled at him not to get injured as he already had been, as she ducked behind the ancient loading crane.

Arc and Pleia watched in horror.

Arc shut his eyes for a moment with a groan.

"Why must they get us from one pancake into another?"

"Frying pan, frying pan," Pleia said, but her mind was on the scene unfolding below them. "We need to take them out of danger before I can purge Ahknett, and I'm unable to purge her from here!"

"So . . . should I climb the crane and jump on its head?" Arc asked gravely.

Pleia gave him a look.

"No, Arc, that's reckless! That's something Dianthe . . . would do . . ."

It began to strike her that the missing Dianthe and Dà-El were related, and no sooner had she had the thought than that missing maiden appeared, perched on the crane, and did exactly that.

"Dianthe!"

Arc and Pleia tried not to facepalm in unison and failed.

Ahknett snapped her neck back with a shriek, giving Eridan and Trissa space to run, and Pleia the opening she needed.

"Get up here, drop the cloak, Tri!" Arc shouted, and Eridan herded Trissa up the wall at a run, clearing it as Dianthe was shaken from her perch and plummeted. She slid down the finned neck into the water, in dangerous reach of Ahknett's flippers, more than her head.

Pleia dropped from the wall, Arc with her, heart pounding. Trissa was left on the wall as Eridan ran to rescue his third charge from the water.

Pleia cast the starlight into the water, flooding the bay, bending her will against Ahknett's, against the shrieks which threatened to stun Dianthe and send her sinking. The waves pushed the maiden away from the beast and she began to swim away, unnoticed, for Ahknett's eyes were on the star.

Voices breathed in Pleia's ear, and she drew back her hand.

"She remembers the song," she realized wonderingly, and began to sing.

Ahknett raised her head at the sound and breathed a soft whistle, drawing closer to the quay as her frill slowly draped against her neck. The head slowly sank down, level with Pleia. The steamy vapor of the pleisiasaur's breath enveloped her, and Pleia stretched out her hand to touch the ridged nose.

The flare of chartreuse and crimson crept back from the seven starmarks, rolling back from eye and frill, leaving there ocean and earth once again.

Ahknett trilled softly, the marks shifting hues, and pushed her nose closer to Pleia.

Pleia's companions felt the tension leaving them with a sigh. Dianthe, chilled and achy from her swim, reached the end of the dock and Eridan lifted her ashore.

"Are we done yet?" Trissa begged. She was leaning shakily on her brother's shoulder.

Both men were tense because they already knew the answer.

Pleia touched Trissa's arm sympathetically but could feel the clock ticking.

She turned back to the horizon as the wind began to whip the bay into froth and foam. Now the gale was whirling around them, forcing them back from the water as Ahknett ducked below the surface for shelter. A cyclonic haze began to form, maddeningly citrine.

The waves were piling ever higher, until it was clear that the cyclone was forming a wall of water all around the island, bursting the thinning mist and flinging it back.

Pleia felt a painful pulse, for the red disc was scarcely in view above the cresting sea.

Arc gripped Pleia's arm, yet his eyes were deeply trusting.

"Save us, Princess."

The mist that was holding the poison back was breaking, and before Pleia drew her next breath, the sun snapped and fell, drinking the light out of the sea and sucking it from the rooftops.

For one instant, Pleia felt her insides turn to ice and she looked helplessly to Arc. He pressed her hand, eyes untroubled.

"I trust you! Trust the angels, if not yourself."

Pleia cast her hand upwards as a tearing sound signaled the breaking of the mist.

A surge of color ran over her, flickering rainbow hues as Ascheré's power coursed through her, against the power which was now hurling shipwreckage at the shoreline. Her companions were dangerously exposed even on the high walls, now that the sea fell so high.

She lashed out with her hand and a beam of white flame burst and burned, skimming the cityline and striking the rent of mist, sealing the milkiness over before the poison could escape. With her left she cast the shield of promise, flinching as she felt the weight of water and wreck crashing against it.

Volatile as it was, finding itself thwarted, the poison cloud descended upon Pleia full-force, endeavoring to drown her before its chance was lost.

Antaré, or something like him, but far more physical darkness now, burst through the cloud and struck her.

"Shall I let you trap me here?" he snarled, and any semblance to Antaré sank into a void of infernality as he towered over her. A single smote from his hand would have annihilated her, and her companions were sealed outside the cyclone, with problems of their own -

Yet, she could neither release the beam nor drop the shield over her companions.

The poison, too, threw its weight upon her as it had upon Arc. Beneath the star's shielding power, she felt frightened, crushed inwards, unable to breathe. Mentally, she clung to the promises made by the seven who had bestowed their gifts upon her, as she was pushed back.

Antaré's onslaught weakened the thin shield surrounding her, and she was thrust back to the edge of the harbor wall.

Her foot slipped and with a heart-wrenching jerk, she plummeted, barely catching herself with her right hand. But she couldn't move to climb, or the beam would break.

If she did, the poison-blight would be freed.

Celae and her sisters would fall.

Her world would die.

XIX

Sorcery

Pleia hung helplessly as the cyclone nearly ripped her from the wall while Antaré's shadow threatened to break her hold. Feverish visions made her half-certain she was endlessly drowning in the sickening waves which surged below her.

"Pleia!"

Arc was on the landing wall just beside and below her, clinging to the stonework as he leaned out.

"I can't; it'll let the poison through," she gasped dazedly. Her arm was burning.

Arc grimaced, and searching for a higher hold, swung himself up onto the plaza ledge.

Antaré turned on him, well two heads higher than Arc. Arc didn't seem to notice.

"*Keep away from her.*"

Each syllable was pronounced as a strike of ice upon ice.

"Can you even try?"

But the laughter in Antaré's eyes died as he looked at the fire in Arc's, and he fell into vexation. He moved to crush Pleia's hand before Arc could strike, but found his limbs impaled by the thorn-darts Arc had released.

Antaré screamed at him and flung the thorns away. Arc ducked and dodged Antaré's oncoming blows.

"Pleia, I need you to drop the shield! They'll be alright, you need more power!"

She dropped it and the glow from her scar surged in brightness.

Antaré was briefly blinded. His physicality waned - Arc bashed him with his spear and toppled him over the edge.

Arc dropped, ducking under the beam, and seizing Pleia's wrist, lifted her to safety.

Dropping the shield had not come without cost, for now their companions found thorns sprouting around them and great seaweed tentacles lashing out at the water's edge, slithering through the harbor, riddled by arrows from Trissa's bow.

Dianthe had been struck down as Eridan hacked at each grasping vine that came towards them; but as soon as one was eliminated, another appeared from the wall of water, and so the seemingly endless cycle ran on –

Trissa dragged Dianthe out of harm's way, and she ran down to join him, drawing her knives and striking out. Thorns threaten to impale them, forcing them to jump every other moment, and soon there was nowhere for them to go.

A growl sounded from behind them.

"Oh no," Eridan muttered with a sinking feeling.

The bears had returned, sprouted undamaged from the cloud.

One charged through the thorns, ramming its way through an arched cloister, and tore all the columns in one strike, throwing them at the pair!

Shards and blocks of stone rained on them, and one pillar threw Eridan against the wall and pinned him there, leaving Trissa helpless, blood running down her face.

"You dare to fall again, *watch me destroy you the way I didn't*," she snarled.

Trissa was forced to hope that she could fend off any moves toward either of them, and that she could hold out at least until Scier decided to take these creatures in hand, or flood the city, leaving them all drowned.

But that didn't matter. She could burn them and shatter their blackened hearts, melting them to resin.

Warrior. . . breathe!

Her eyes widened as she watched the oncoming titans. This was not the way. Arc had saved her once before. She couldn't save herself.

"Aaaarc!"

He heard her cry and turned, at a loss.

"Go to her!" Pleia commanded, and he leapt down the wall.

But the bears hadn't been heading for Trissa. They were only looking for a stepping-stone. They'd found it in the shattered wreckage, giving them room to climb.

"No, you're *not* going to touch her!" Arc growled, and barred the way.

Sealing the rift wasn't putting the poison closer to purged. Risky, but she could train her power upon the cloud and its visages instead –

She changed the aim of the beam, and it burned like plasma-light on metal, compressing the cloud around her.

It was good, but was it enough?

No, she knew without asking that she needed to sing as she always had, but whenever her lips parted, the mist strove to choke her, filling her mind with its visions and disrupting the recollection she needed.

Light sparked beside her and Ascheré, Tiran and Ireo stood beside her, and it was the light of their eyes that burned.

Ascheré's sword cut at the mist, which was binding Pleia, and he drew her back behind his shield.

"Stay with me, little star."

Ireo's hand supported the aching arm which Pleia could scarcely keep raised. His glare lifted for a reassuring smile as Tiran's light encompassed her.

"Breathe with me, little one," she heard him say, and it was as though the light gave her a place to rest, keeping her power from falling, boosting it to where it needed to be.

Pleia's eyes went through the mist to where Arc was, and for a moment her horror dimmed the beam as she saw his predicament.

The bears were too poisoned to heed his voice, so he had taken them on to protect her.

His face was already bleeding from their claws, but in that one instant that her eyes were fastened upon him, he had pulled both titans into the seaweed's grasp, and all three were dragged into the water wall.

"No!" Ascheré said gently. "Concentrate! You haven't lost him, Pleia!"

Her heart felt stabbed open to bleeding as she tried to focus her eyes on the poison yawning around her. It was the only way to save him.

She relinquished her hold on the beam and closed her eyes, feeling the spinning sensation cease, as though she were too dizzy to feel; letting the vision of Maia and Scier float before her, she began to sing their names, dimming the roar around her.

The pulse beat faster, not wanting to lose its hold. There were no sounds more powerful than these sacred names, a grace so simple it took the end of the world to find it.

Pleia opened her eyes and sang with her soul. A sound like the rushing of the tide and wall crashed against wall, fog upon mist.

The thundering cyclonic roar was sucked into a whisper and faded, leaving Pleia momentarily in the vacuum of silence. The rock rumbled beneath her feet, shuddering.

She put her hand to the ground, and with the angels, smashed and sealed the rifts that lay deep beneath the sea, buried in the bedrock of the hill.

All at once a mist none of them had sensed lifted, as if it were a prison door, and the whisperings Pleia had heard and the vague faces faded into silence, finally at rest.

Pleia looked into the night sky as the vacuum collapsed, her vision full of star-crested waves and tender-eyed angels, and she crumpled.

She couldn't see a thing, now, and was too worn to move; the arms that caught her told her that all she'd feared was only that, and that her companions were safe.

As the last shred of mist cleared over the palace walls, Celae and her sister kingdoms were safe, at last, too.

The star ebbed from her brow. The pearl faded, leaving Pleia wan and weary.

Only a chain of diamonds, like a star, remained around her neck. Diamonds, and yet not, for nothing but the Star of Bethel had ever sparkled the way they did.

The sound of the waves and her companions' voices came back to Pleia; including one that was unfamiliar.

"Is she alright?" Dianthe was asking. She had recovered from the thorns that had put her to sleep.

"Only vidéstad."

"Celaean, please."

"Exhausted.'"

Pleia opened her eyes.

"Arc?" she mumbled.

"I'm here."

He was there, albeit dripping wet. He rubbed her shoulder gently.

"I'm here, thanks to your pleisiasaur, Pleia."

Ahknett's head was resting on the flat near them, her breath warming them from the water's chill.

Eridan was kneeling beside them, a purpling welt over his jaw. Pleia reached for him with a frown and tried to cover it with her hand, but he stopped her.

"It's alright, little star. It's not that bad."

She began to realize that the poison – and her gift – was gone, that the feverish torment had been just that. She slowly sat up from where she lay on Arc's shoulder. Dianthe and Trissa were behind her, both damp and with their share of bruises, but nothing serious.

"I want to go home and sleep."

"We'll spend the night now," Eridan said, stroking her hair. "We'll find someplace that maybe isn't so damp or full of broken windows and start home in the morning."

"Noooo," Trissa groaned, and fell flat backwards on the paving stones at the thought of the return journey.

"Don't have to spend the night," Pleia said sleepily. "The angels can take us."

Ahknett moaned softly. Pleia laid her hand on the inquisitive nose.

"Rest now, Ahknett . . . there's nothing left for you to fight."

The frill fanned and Ahknett trilled Pleia's song, as if to say goodbye. With a sigh, she reluctantly let her head sink below the waves and swam away, leaving the last page of her life to be carved on Alultaurari's ancient walls of memory.

"Is it just me, or is the ocean sinking?" Dianthe asked abruptly.

"I hope it's just you," Eridan replied, but it wasn't; the ocean was, indeed, falling back, gradually revealing the once-inhabited regions.

Rather, the still-inhabited regions.

Most of the ocean remained as it had been, but Alultaurari's hill was revealed, and the kingdom's plain. They wouldn't know it until the morning, but islands had likewise formed near the shores of Rada and Adar.

"Think I need my eyes checked," Trissa commented, blaming it on exhaustion. "Lights?"

"Oh yes, those," was Arc's reply, as though they were nothing new, and the intact village was nothing unusual, for he'd seen them when he'd nearly drowned.

"The reason for the breathable layer of the sea," Pleia explained. "Those outside the city were preserved by the sea before the poison could take them. Now they are free, too."

Arc assisted her to her feet. Light was shimmering behind them; Pleia twisted her head to find the portal that was awaiting them, beyond which they could dimly see warmly lit rooms. Eridan took Dianthe and Trissa by the arm, and they walked each other through; Arc and Pleia followed, with one last glance to the stars overhead.

It was Tygeta which lay on the other side, strangely aglow with life. Someone saw them and pulled them quickly onto the palace balcony, where Lady Elnath stood, overlooking Celae. She was surprised at their appearance, but detailed to them that Celae was safe; something about an averted invasion, but the travelers were bone-tired enough that it didn't register.

Taking pity on them, Elnath sent them off to various guest chambers. They were only glad to have the rest they'd been missing. They fell asleep to a song they had come to know well, as the Pleiades once again drifted westward, wrapped in their heavenly mist.

XX

Rhapsody

It was strange to wake up in Tygeta on the morrow. Pleia sat up in bed, searching her sleep-fogged memory. What brought it back was her fingers finding the diamonds still hung about her neck. She slipped out of bed at once to pray and dress in an autumn robe she found in the wardrobe.

A walk through the halls didn't locate her companions, until she stepped into a private cloistered garden and found Arc sitting up high on a mossy wall, gazing at the azured sky. He, too, wore the change of clothing provided, layered in blue and brown, appearing no worse for wear. His face seemed restful now, in a way she hadn't seen before. His eyes lit up when he saw her, and he helped her climb up beside him.

"I didn't dream you," Pleia said, putting her arms around him.

He smiled contentedly.

"Know what else you didn't dream?"

He told her what Elnath had tried to relay to them upon their arrival: that at the very moment of the poison's purging, Celae had been spared of an invasion which would have crushed her like a swarm of locusts after a drought.

Elnath had been warned of an attack planned on Celae the previous evening; armies had gathered at the borders of Uthold, Adar, Rada, Estaria, and Nemaniya, on the boundaries of Archidron. The Guardians never would have been able to hold them back, nor to fight the fire which was set to blaze down the protecting forest. Less so would they have been able to face the poison which would have turned every soul against another. The curse would have claimed Celae, followed by the sea.

But unexplained cloudless rain had ended the flames, wakening the armies in confusion as to why they'd gathered; and coming to Elnath, the leaders had offered to grant Celae a chance under her rule, recognizing that she was not her uncle, but the daughter of the man who had once been their friend.

The border guard was restored on either side, freeing the Guardians of their duties, and the people from fear. The Guardians were free to return whither they would; many were at a loss, but they would find ground again, as they had in exile. As for Arc, he had the only ground he really needed.

"What would I do without you?" Arc whispered.

"I thought it was the other way around?"

He smiled a little and shook his head.

"No, I need you."

Eridan's voice hailed them as he exited the cloister, Trissa on his arm. He looked better; the bruise on his cheek had lightened, and he seemed not to be feeling the muscle-ache.

The couple was trailed by Dianthe, who seemed to be trying to maximize her stealth. Perhaps she didn't wish to explain her troublesome absence the previous day, or perhaps Eridan had scolded her excessively for it.

"Don't be falling, Pleia," Eridan warned from below.

"I believe it's too late," Trissa smiled. "In one way, at least."

"Vërtë, as someone would say."

"Ask him," Pleia urged Arc.

"Eridan, we have a question," Arc announced.

He and Pleia gestured to each other, but Arc beat her to it.

"Whatever would she do without me?"

Pleia grabbed his hands and swatted them playfully, and Arc had to keep her from tumbling.

"That was my line!"

"What do you mean, that was your line? I asked you what you would do without me, and you said we should ask Eridan, so I'm asking Eridan!"

Pleia started laughing, but she was crying, too.

"Oh, come on," Arc murmured, folding her in his arms. "Poor thing, you've been through so much lately."

"Are you saying the rest of you haven't? You all almost got eaten by a giant fish thing or bloodthirsty seaweed," Pleia choked, half laughing.

"Pssh, I never doubted you for a moment; you, you doubted yourself for about. . . oh, three million seconds."

"I can confirm," Eridan laughed softly, offering no comment on the question asked, and turned the talk to all that Arc had told Pleia.

When pressed, Dianthe recounted, with some discomfort under Eridan's stern glance, her absence.

"I was following you, again," she admitted to Pleia. "Only. . . I found Antaré before I found you. He imprisoned me in a rock cell, and it took me some time to be free. I'd been hearing a sound like thunder, so I followed it to the harbor, where I found you."

She shrugged when asked why she had leapt upon Ahknett and confessed that certainly she'd already known of Dà-El's deeds through various family heirlooms and accounts. Not to mention, she revealed, that Elnath was her aunt.

As far as she was concerned, leaping onto a pleisiasaur's neck was the natural route to take.

What she hadn't known was, firstly, of Pleia's ancestry, whereupon the pair ecstatically realized they were cousins; and secondly, the question of why, regarding Antaré's presence.

"I made inquiries, and you can be certain that Antaré is safely in asylum," Arc informed her. "It would seem the entirety of yesterday he was screaming in his cell . . . something about Guardians and Star-Brights and pleisiasaurs . . ."

"Possessed by the poison he nearly unleashed," Trissa surmised. "And his appearance, to the three of you then, might be that he was your worst fear, as I found mine, and I think I accidentally brought Eri's."

Eridan squeezed her shoulders.

"Failing as a guardian to you three, and losing you, would have been, little Tri."

It wasn't long until Elnath herself came to them, inviting the five to morning tea, offering further information on the state of the Kingdom. Once she'd heard the tale they had to tell, she offered any expression of gratitude they desired.

All they wanted was to go home, avoiding the public eye, and to know what they were to do with their lives now that their known purposes had been fulfilled.

Elnath acquiesced, but seemed reluctant to direct any of them, particularly Pleia.

"The maidens, such as little Dianthe, will be returning home now, of course," Elnath said to Eridan.

"Yes. I must be getting back to assist," he replied gravely. "I'll be needed to sign their release of vows and coordinate with their families."

Elnath arranged for horses to be brought later that morning, and by early afternoon, the group was dismounting in the Temple courtyard. It was abuzz with families reuniting with their daughters.

One by one, Eridan signed each maiden's release of vows and returned her to her family.

"Alright, Pleia, let's get you signed off," Eridan sighed at last, delivering the last girl down the stairs. He drew Pleia up them.

"But 'Dan, I have no place else to go," Pleia protested.

"Imagine that, I have no place else to go, either, and I'm signing myself off, too."

He squeezed her hand.

"Mm, we Guardians have no place to go, either, 'cept Nazar," Arc mused, watching as Eridan stamped the release once Pleia had put her name to it.

Pleia straightened, feeling both free and lost.

Dianthe laughed, perched on the banister, waiting for her father to finish with the priests.

"What sort of trouble are you giving me, Dia?" Eridan inquired, not raising his eyes. He passed the papers to the mother superior and the process was complete: Pleia was adrift.

"Well, I know of a place that's about to have kingdoms fight over it, that is, if you're not careful."

She grinned mischievously. "I highly recommend you talk to my aunt, before someone else does."

"Oh no," Trissa stared at the wall. "Not again."

"I think we'd best speak to Lady Elnath. . ." Arc muttered.

So it was that the group returned to Tygeta, whereupon Elnath and Eridan placed Pleia under Arc's guardianship via engagement, to both his confusion and honor.

"Arcturus Kitai Tähevǎli, I place Pleia Aldebaran within your guardianship. And you'd better keep her safe, or I am *not* bringing dessert to your wedding," Eridan threatened.

Pleia looked up to Arc, her hands having been placed in his, and felt safe again.

"That answers that question," Arc managed to say.

"Do you have another one?" Elnath wondered.

"Many, but how about the question of my sister," and Arc surrendered Trissa to Eridan's guardianship, with a, "And, Eridan Cadoret, if you don't do this right, I am *not* bringing the cake to your wedding, either, you'll receive seaweed!"

Which, considering their history with seaweed, was a decidedly disastrous event to contemplate.

Amidst navigating this turn of events, the couples likewise received Elnath's blessing to see what could be done to ensure Alultaurari's safe reclamation, if the previously undersea inhabitants should allow them to do so.

The trip meant reuniting with Ur and Ceri after their riders' long absence, and taking a far more comfortable route through what was now friendly territory. They found the bridge permanently raised to meet them; permanently, in so far as they discovered the secret mechanism in the palace, which could be used to submerge it to protect the city.

After some negotiating, the villagers were, in fact, relieved to have a safe connection to the outside modern world after centuries of isolation.

The travelers were happy to find a titan-sized surprise waiting for them in the harbor that first day: seemingly Ahknett's orphaned infant, she was christened Minazal, becoming a true tagalong to Pleia, in so far as she was able.

Wedding preparations were made alongside the moving of the Guardians, and by the spring, wedding bells were rung, and soon after, Alultaurari became a city once more. Somehow, no one was surprised when Dianthe appeared, dragging her family along on a permanent visit.

There seemed only one option of leadership, when that time came, for no one would think otherwise than to place Pleia upon the throne, Arc at her side, the ancient crowns of their predecessors upon their brows. Eridan was raised into Aldebaran's position as the city champion, and Dianthe followed in Gienna's footsteps.

In only a matter of months, Alultaurari's glory was restored, her streets alive, her borders safe; interest in her history came from the kingdoms surrounding her, and she was strengthened by their friendship.

Buildings were repaired, wreckage cleared, and the city whitewashed. The angels' statues were recarved and repainted, the cathedral filled with song, the palace mended, and Alultaurari's customs brought back to light.

The city's tarnished memories began to find new flowers: the story which had sadly ceased to be written was carved upon the columns, crowned by the tale of the Star-bearer and her hero. The Starpool's song continued, mingled with the laughter of children playing in the Hall of Maia.

Little Ayeleth had a sister now; this time, she was safe with Eridan. As for Arc and Pleia's children, something of the Pleiades seemed to be in their eyes.

Maybe, now, the people would be safe; maybe, they'd remain with Scier. But Pleia knew that if they fell again, the Light of Starra would find them, for the love of Scier was as eternal as the westward winding river of the Pleiades.